HARLEQUIN®
Presents

Welcome to the October 2008 collection of
Harlequin Presents!

This month read Sandra Marton's *The Sheikh's
Defiant Bride,* the first book in her exciting
trilogy THE SHEIKH TYCOONS. We also visit
the Mediterranean, and two affluent heroes who
aren't afraid to take what they want, in Julia James's
Greek Tycoon, Waitress Wife and Robyn Donald's
His Majesty's Mistress. Things begin to heat up at
work (or should we say *after* work) for Abby in
Anne Oliver's *Business in the Bedroom.* Maggie Cox
also brings you a sexy office tale, this time involving
an Italian tycoon and his unsuspecting personal
assistant, in *Secretary Mistress, Convenient Wife.*
Helen Bianchin weaves a story of attraction and
convenience in *Purchased: His Perfect Wife,* in
which cash-strapped Lara finds herself making a
deal with her brooding stepbrother. Innocence is
lost and passion abounds in *One Night with His
Virgin Mistress* by Sara Craven, and housekeeper
Liv's job description is more hands-on than most
in *Housekeeper at His Beck and Call,* compliments
of Susan Stephens.

We'd love to hear what you think about
Harlequin Presents. E-mail us at
Presents@hmb.co.uk, or join in the
discussions at ww
www.sensationalr
you'll also find mo
books and authors

D1012074

Bedded by...
Blackmail
Forced to bed...then to wed?

He's got her firmly in his sights and she's got
only one chance for survival—surrender to his
blackmail...and him...in his bed!

Bedded by...Blackmail!

The *big* miniseries from Harlequin Presents®

Dare you read it?

Julia James

GREEK TYCOON, WAITRESS WIFE

Bedded by... 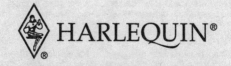 *Blackmail*
Forced to bed...then to wed?

◆ HARLEQUIN®

TORONTO • NEW YORK • LONDON
AMSTERDAM • PARIS • SYDNEY • HAMBURG
STOCKHOLM • ATHENS • TOKYO • MILAN • MADRID
PRAGUE • WARSAW • BUDAPEST • AUCKLAND

ISBN-13: 978-0-373-12764-1
ISBN-10: 0-373-12764-2

GREEK TYCOON, WAITRESS WIFE

First North American Publication 2008.

Printed in U.S.A.

All about the author...
Julia James

JULIA JAMES lives in England with her family.
Harlequin® novels were the first "grown-up" books
she read as a teenager, alongside Georgette Heyer
and Daphne du Maurier, and she's been reading them
ever since. Julia adores the British countryside in all
its seasons, and is fascinated by all things historical,
from castles to cottages. She also has a special love for
the Mediterranean—"the most perfect landscape after
England!" She considers both ideal settings for romance
stories! Since becoming a romance writer, she has, she
says, had the great good fortune to start discovering the
Caribbean as well, and is happy to report that those
magical, beautiful islands are also ideal settings for
romance stories. "One of the best things about writing
romance is that it gives you a great excuse to take
holidays in fabulous places," says Julia, "all in the name of
research, of course!"

Her first stab at novel-writing was Regency romances.
"But, alas, no one wanted to publish them," she says.
She put her writing aside until her family commitments
were clear, and then renewed her love affair with
contemporary romances. "My writing partner and I
made a pact not to give up until we were published—
and we both succeeded! Natasha Oakley writes for the
Harlequin Romance line, and we faithfully read each
other's works in progress and give each other a lot of
free advice and encouragement."

When not writing, Julia enjoys walking, gardening,
needlework, baking "extremely gooey chocolate cakes"
and trying to stay fit!

CHAPTER ONE

ALEXEIS NICOLAIDES glanced around him with displeasure. It had been a mistake to come here. A mistake to indulge Marissa. He was only in London for a twenty-four-hour stop-over, and when he'd got out of the day-long meeting in the City and returned to his hotel suite he'd simply wanted to find her waiting for him. Then, once the bare niceties had been dispensed with, and they had made polite and completely empty enquiries about each other's well-being, he would have done what his fundamental interest in Marissa was: taken her to bed. Instead, however, he had ended up in this overcrowded art gallery, bored rigid and surrounded by yapping idiots—among whom Marissa was the key offender. At this moment she was giving full throat to her knowledge of the art market and the financial worth of the artist on display. Alexeis couldn't have cared less about either.

And with every passing moment he was caring less and less about Marissa, and about spending any more time with her. Not here—and not even in bed.

Even as he stood there, an expression of growing irritation in his eyes, he made his decision. Marissa was going to have to go. Up till now she hadn't been much of a problem—no more than any woman was, for they all, invariably, wanted

to outstay their shelf-life with him. But three months on
Marissa, savvy as well as beddable, was evidently starting
to think she could start making demands. Like insisting he
take her to this opening. Doubtless she thought that an
absence of a fortnight would have whetted his appetite for
her so much that he would be complaisant to her whims.

His dark eyes narrowed.

Mistake. His was not a complaisant nature. The Nicolaides
wealth had always meant that he could call the shots when it
came to women. He chose the ones he wanted and then they
did what he wanted—or they were out. No matter how beautiful, how desirable, how highly they rated themselves.

Marissa Harcourt rated herself very highly. She was fero-
ciously chic, with head-turning looks, a well-connected background, an Oxbridge degree and a fashionable and highly
paid career in the art world. Clearly she considered these at-
tributes sufficient not just to attach herself to a man like
himself, but to hold him.

Did she even, Alexeis found himself speculating, consider
them sufficient to hold him permanently?

Her predecessor had thought so. Adrianna Garsoni, whose
exotic looks, soaring soprano voice and talent for self-pro-
motion ensured her status as a diva at La Scala, had clearly
believed that marrying Alexeis would mean the rich
Nicolaides coffers could be put to work furthering her career.
The moment Adrianna had shown her hand, making it clear
she considered that marriage was on the agenda, Alexeis had
disposed of her. Her reaction had been volatile in the extreme,
but irrelevant to him. In comparison with Adrianna's tempes-
tuous personality, Alexeis had welcomed Marissa's cool chic,
as well as enjoying her highly sensual nature in bed.

Now, it seemed, much to his irritation, she would have to
go too. He had quite enough going on in his life as it was.

Alexeis's thoughts shifted closer to home, and mouth tightened automatically. His father was currently marrying his fifth wife, and far too busy to bother himself with the intricacies and pressure of running a global business. As for his half-brother, Yannis, he was the offspring of his father's second marriage, and far too busy pursuing his twin pleasures in life—fast sports and faster women. Alexeis's mouth tightened even more.

However, he knew that the last thing he'd welcome was his father trying to interfere in how he was running the group, or Yannis trying to muscle in on it. The latter, at least, was one thing upon which Alexeis saw eye to eye with his mother. Berenice Nicolaides was vehement in her determination that the son of the woman who had usurped her should not get his hands on what she considered her own son's rightful inheritance—nothing less than total and permanent control of the Nicolaides Group. Alexeis's reason for wanting Yannis out of the picture was less vindictive—he merely considered his brother feckless, hedonistic, and far too much of a risk to be involved in running so large and complex a company.

Alexeis didn't always agree with his mother. And on one aspect of his inheritance he was completely at odds with her. Alexeis's eyes darkened as they always did when his thoughts were called in that unwelcome direction. Berenice was convinced—obsessed, he amended—that he should marry an heiress, preferably Greek-born, both to bolster his own financial position and to present his father with a grandson to continue the Nicolaides dynasty. Her constant attempts to matchmake only exasperated Alexeis.

As did, right now, Marissa's discoursing on the art market. He made some perfunctory reply, still considering whether to end their relationship right now. The trouble was, if he did, he would be facing yet another night on his own. The dilemma worsened his mood and, peremptorily, he beckoned to a server circulating with drinks. As his fingers circled the stem of a champagne flute, he found himself glancing at her.

And holding the glance.

Long, blonde hair, caught back in a clip at her nape, an oval face with flawless features, translucent skin, a short straight nose and accented cheekbones. Wide-set, long-lashed clear grey eyes completed the package—the very delectable package. His first thought was automatic. What was a girl with looks like that doing working as a waitress?

He took the glass, murmuring a thank-you, and the girl's eyes met his.

He could see it happen as if in slow motion: her reaction to him. Her reaction to the way he was looking at her.

The soft grey-blue eyes widened, pupils dilating and her lips parted slightly. For one long moment she looked—helpless. That was the word, thought Alexeis. As if there was nothing she could do except meet his eyes and let him look at her.

Out of nowhere, Alexeis felt his mood improve. She really was very, very lovely—

'There's no mineral water.'

Marissa's voice was a snap of complaint. Suddenly the waitress looked flustered. Her eyes broke from Alexeis, and went to the woman at his side.

'I—I'm very sorry,' she stammered.

She had a low voice, Alexeis noted, and sounded nervous and under stress. The tray, crowded with brimming glasses, wobbled slightly in her uplifted hands.

Marissa rasped in irritation. 'Well, don't just stand there like a dummy. Go and get some. Still, not sparkling—and no lemon.'

The girl swallowed. 'Yes, yes, of course,' she got out.

Jerkily, she turned to go. As she did, another of the guests in the crowded gallery stepped back abruptly and collided with her. Instinctively Alexeis felt his hand go out to balance the tray in the girl's hands, but it was too late. The glass of orange juice nearest the edge tottered crazily and then cascaded forwards, smashing to the ground and emptying its contents all over Marissa's cocktail dress.

'You *idiot*!' Marissa's voice was shrill with fury. 'Just *look* what you've done!'

A look of horror—and more—convulsed the girl's face.

'I'm…I'm sorry—' It was all she could get out.

A space had cleared around her, and someone was bustling up to her. A short man with an expression on his face that was both irate, and aghast.

'What's going on here?' he demanded.

'Isn't it *obvious?*' Marissa's voice was still shrill. 'This *moron* has *ruined* my dress.'

The aghast look on the short man's face deepened, and he launched into vociferous apology—which Alexeis cut short.

'Only the bodice is wet, Marissa,' he said coolly, cutting the man off. 'If you sponge it down it will dry out. It's dark; it won't show.'

Marissa was not consoled. 'You half-brained little *idiot*!' she raged at the girl again.

Alexeis put a restraining hand on her wrist. 'Go and find the powder room,' he said. It wasn't a suggestion.

Throwing him a fulminating glance, Marissa stormed off. Meantime, the short man had summoned two other waiting staff, who'd rushed up with cloths and a dustpan and brush, to clear up the shards and the spilt juice on the polished wood floor. He'd also banished the erring waitress whilst Alexeis had spoken to Marissa. Alexeis could see her scurrying, shoulders hunched, towards the back of the gallery.

Then the short man was turning his fulsomely dismayed apologies on Alexeis. Alexeis wasn't interested. 'It was an accident,' he said curtly, nodding dismissal impatiently.

The moment was too opportune to miss—he strode to the reception desk at the entrance.

'Tell Ms Harcourt I've had to leave,' he said. Then he walked out of the gallery, extracting his mobile to summon his driver. He'd send Marissa a cheque for a new dress, and a trinket to wear with it. it. That should dispose of her. It also meant he'd be facing a celibate night for certain.

Without volition, he found himself thinking about the waitress Marissa had railed at. He frowned—there had been no call to be so abusive to the girl. It had been an accident, not incompetence. His mind wandered back to his perusal of the girl. She really had been very lovely indeed. And in the black, tight-skirted, white-aproned outfit, with the close-fitting short-sleeved white blouse, she'd looked very—

Beddable—that was the word for it.

Oh, not too obviously, not too flagrantly, but there was no denying that the black and white uniform—together with her soft blondeness and those long-lashed wide-set eyes—did the business.

Involuntarily, he felt himself tightening.

Damn—that was *not* an appropriate response right now! However lovely she was, the girl was not the type of female he usually consorted with. Anyway, he was not in the habit of picking women up on a casual basis. He selected them carefully, not just on their looks, but on whether they would fit into his lifestyle—and, of course, not seek to outstay their shelf-life.

His car glided up to the pavement and he got in. Tonight he would just have to work, that was all. He was flying to New York in the morning anyway, and he knew a large selection of suitable women there from which to choose a replacement for Marissa.

He sat back in the moulded leather seat, looking indifferently out of the tinted window as the car moved forward, heading back down Bond Street. It took him past the gallery again, and he was relieved to see no sign of Marissa. He felt his conscience twinge at having ended their relationship so ruthlessly, but put it aside. He knew very well that the main attraction for her was his wealth and status—nothing more.

He was about to avert his gaze when a figure caught his eye. Walking along with a rapid, somehow jerky gait, shoulders hunched, blonde head bowed, raincoat wrapped tightly round her, hands in pockets and shoulder bag clutched to her side, was the waitress.

Abruptly, for no reason he could justify, Alexeis pressed the intercom button.

'Stop the car,' he ordered his driver.

CHAPTER TWO

CARRIE kept walking forward. If she kept walking, she wouldn't think. Wouldn't think she'd just lost her job. Again. Was she doomed to keep losing jobs? she thought woefully. It had been her own fault, obviously, and she couldn't blame them for sacking her. She'd let herself be distracted, she knew—fatally—by that incredible man. If she hadn't been gawping at him so stupidly she'd have been more aware of what was going on. But, no, she'd had to just stand there like an idiot.

She hadn't been able to help herself, though. He had just been so *incredible*! It really was the only word for him. She'd never seen a man that good-looking, who had that kind of impact. Talk about tall, dark and handsome! In the few moments she'd looked at him she hadn't really been able to take in any specific details, but the overall impact had been just amazing.

And when he'd met her eyes…

She felt again the whoosh that had knocked her in that breathless moment, when she'd felt the impact of those dark, long-lashed eyes holding hers. There had been something in them as he'd looked at her that had squeezed her lungs tight.

Then his partner had wanted water, and the moment had passed. And then—then the disaster.

Mr Bartlett had raged at her when he'd found her in the back, and sacked her on the spot. She was incredibly lucky, he'd told her, not to have to pay for the woman's dress she'd ruined, which would easily have cost hundreds of pounds. Even so she'd been sacked without her wages, to cover the cost of the specialist dry cleaning Mr Bartlett had said would be required.

Well, at least now she could get a daytime job and not just the evening work that she'd been restricted to up till now. Her eyes shadowed. She'd only been in London for three months, and had been glad to get away from her home—get away from the grief and the anguished memory of her father's final days. Glad, too, to get away from everyone's sympathy, not to mention the kindly meant offers of financial help that she could never accept. Here, in this vast city, she was all but anonymous, and she welcomed it.

Yet London was a bleak place, certainly when finances were as straitened as hers were. Just keeping her head above water was hard, but it had to be done—at least until the summer was over and she could go home again to Marchester and resume the life she knew, painful though it would be without her father. Casual jobs here, at least, were plentiful, but it was relentless and grinding, and in three months she'd had no time off for herself and no money to spare for anything beyond necessities.

There was another aspect to working in London she didn't like either. The hassle she got. That was what had cost her the first job she'd lost. She'd been working in a tapas bar and a customer had slid his hand up her skirt. Shocked and appalled, she had hit his hand away violently. The man had complained about her and Carrie had been sacked. The woman at the job agency had been unsympathetic.

'With your looks you should be used to it—and used to handling it,' she'd said dismissively.

But she wasn't, thought Carrie miserably. No one behaved like that in the world she was used to, nor had any interest in doing so. Their minds were focussed on other matters. It was hard to be subjected to that kind of treatment, or even just to be looked at the way men did here—so blatantly. So sleazily.

It wasn't sleazy when that incredible guy looked at you—

Memory flushed through her again hotly. No, sleazy had not been the word. Not in the slightest. The way that man had looked at her had made her feel—

Breathless.

She felt the tightness in her chest again as she recalled the way his eyes had held hers. He really had been amazing! The sort of fantasy man a girl could dream about. He was probably rich, too, because all the guests at the gallery had been—or at least well-heeled. He'd had a very rich look indeed about him. There'd been something about him, something more than just his fantastic dark looks and what had obviously been a hand-made suit and a silk tie—a sort of assurance, arrogance, even, as if he were one of the princes of the world…

She gave a twist of her mouth. Whatever he was, he belonged to the London that she didn't! The one she only saw from the other side of the bar or the table or through the door, where the likes of her served the likes of him, and remained anonymous and unobtrusive.

Dejection hit her again, and she quickened her pace, unconsciously hunching her shoulders, feeling bleak and lonely. Though she saved money and got exercise by walking, there was still a good long way back to the poky bedsit in Paddington that was all she could afford.

Suddenly she stopped. A car door had just opened in front of her, enough to block her path and require her to veer around it. Then, as she gathered her wits to do just that, a voice spoke.

'Are you all right?'

Carrie's head turned. The voice—deep, and with an accent she did not register—came from the interior of the car. As she looked at the speaker her eyes widened involuntarily. It was the incredible-looking man from the gallery, whose girlfriend's dress she'd soaked. Apprehension stabbed at her. Was he going to demand money for the dress? She didn't have anywhere near enough on her, even just for cleaning it. And if he told her she had to replace it she would be completely stuck. The prospect was so daunting that she just froze.

The man was getting out of the car, and she stepped back hurriedly. He seemed taller than she remembered—and even more incredible looking. She couldn't help reacting to it, even though it was the stupidest thing in the world to do.

'Is—is it about the dress?' she blurted, gripping her bag by its shoulder strap out of sheer tension.

A frown pleated his brow momentarily. It made him look even more forbidding than the dark, severely tailored bespoke suit and his air of wealth and power did.

'Your girlfriend's dress? The one I spilt the juice over?' Carrie continued.

The man ignored her question. 'Why are you not still at the gallery?' he demanded.

Carrie swallowed. It seemed more like an accusation than a question, and she could only say, 'I got dismissed.'

The man said something in a language she did not recognise. He looked foreign, she registered belatedly. That dark tanned skin and the darker eyes.

'You were fired?' he demanded. Again, it sounded like an accusation.

Carrie could only nod, and clutch her bag more tightly.

'I'm really sorry about the dress. Mr Bartlett said he'd use my wages to dry clean it, so I hope it will be all right.'

The man made an impatient gesture with his hand.

'The dress is taken care of,' he said. 'But tell me—do you want your job back? If you do I shall arrange it. What happened was clearly an accident.'

Carrie felt her cheeks heat with acute embarrassment.

'No—please,' she said. 'I mean—thank you—thank you for offering. And I'm really very sorry about the dress. I really am,' she finished quickly. Then she made to start walking again.

Her elbow was taken.

'Allow me,' said the man, 'to offer you a lift to wherever you are going.' His voice had changed somehow. She didn't know how. It seemed smooth—not abrasive, the way it had been before. Then the import of what he'd said registered. Carrie could only stare at him—feel his hand on her elbow like a burning brand.

'A lift?' she echoed stupidly. 'No—no, thank you. I'm fine walking.'

Something flickered in the man's eyes. If she hadn't known better she would have said it was surprise.

'Nevertheless,' he said. The smoothness was still there, but underpinned now by something else. 'Please—allow me. I insist. After all, it is the least I can do to make amends for you losing your job.'

Carrie's eyes widened even more. 'But it wasn't anything to do with you!'

'Had I been quicker off the mark I could have steadied your tray,' said the man, in the same smooth voice. 'Now, where would you like to be driven?'

The hold on her elbow had tightened imperceptibly, and Carrie felt herself being inexorably guided towards the open door of the car.

'No—please, it's not at all necessary.' Nor, she knew with

strong female instinct, would his girlfriend welcome the presence of the waitress who'd ruined her dress.

'Please do not delay me further. The car is causing an obstruction.' The voice was still smooth, but now in its place was something like impatience.

Carrie looked, and realised that cars were backing up, unable to get by easily. Without realising how, she found herself being handed into the car, looking apprehensively for the brunette. But she wasn't there.

'Where's your girlfriend?' She'd gone back to blurting.

The man lowered himself lithely into the seat next to her, and reached for his seat belt with a fluid movement. He cast a frowning look at Carrie.

'Girlfriend?'

'The one I spilt the juice over—'

His eyes cleared. 'She is not my girlfriend.' He said the word as if it were deeply alien to him.

Something lifted in Carrie. Something she knew was quite pointless, but it did all the same. That chic brunette hadn't been his girlfriend.

And it wouldn't matter if she was, anyway! Good grief, what do you think this is? Some kind of pick-up? For some reason the man feels a sense of obligation that you've lost your job, and is giving you a lift! That's all!

She swallowed again. 'The end of Bond Street will be fine. Thank you very much.'

The man didn't say anything, just instructed the driver to go, and the car moved forward. Carrie sank back into the leather seat. It was deep and luxurious, as was the rest of the car. Carrie had never been inside a car so upmarket, and she couldn't help looking around. The man was leaning forward, depressing a button, and a recessed shelf slid forward into the spacious leg-well between them. Carrie's eyes widened.

There was a bottle of champagne and several flutes. Before she could say or do anything, she was watching with disbelieving fascination as the man lifted the champagne bottle, eased it expertly open, and with equal expertise took up a flute, tilted it, and filled it with foaming liquid. Then he handed it to her.

'Um—' said Carrie. But she found she had taken the flute anyway.

The smallest semblance of a smile seemed to flicker momentarily at the man's mouth, before he filled his own glass and replaced the bottle in its holder. He eased back in his seat again and turned towards Carrie, who was just sitting there, disbelievingly.

'It's very good champagne, I do assure you,' the man said. Again, that smile flickered briefly on his mouth, as if he found her reaction amusing. He took a considering mouthful of the gently effervescing liquid. 'Yes, perfectly drinkable,' he said. 'Try it.'

Carrie lifted the glass to her mouth, and sipped. The chilled pale gold champagne slipped into her mouth, tasting delicious. Her eyes widened. She knew almost nothing about champagne, but she could tell that this was, indeed, a superior potation.

'What do you think of it?' the man asked. The smoothness was in his voice again, and it seemed to glide over Carrie, doing strange things to her. Like getting her to drink a glass of champagne with a man who was a complete stranger.

But we're in the middle of Bond Street! It might be bizarre, but it's not dangerous or anything!

And it was also—irresistible. The word was the right one, she knew, because it summed up what seemed to be going on in her—an inability to resist.

'It's lovely,' she said. She didn't know what else to say, and it was the truth. Gingerly, she took another sip.

I'm drinking champagne with a tall, dark, handsome stranger. It's something that will never happen to me twice in my life, so I might as well make the most of the experience!

'I'm glad you like it,' said the man, as he took another mouthful himself. He eased his long legs forward. His eyes were resting on her, and Carrie felt intensely self-conscious.

Oh, God, he really is gorgeous, she thought helplessly. Beneath his disturbing regard, she felt her nerve-ends jitter. Instinctively, she took another mouthful of the champagne. It fizzed down her throat, its native effervescence seeming to infect her blood.

'So, where would you like to eat tonight?' said the man. The voice was again as smooth as ever.

Carrie stared. 'Eat?'

The man gestured loosely with his half-empty flute. 'Of course,' he said, as if it had been the most logical thing in the world to say to her. The most obvious.

An edge of caution cut into Carrie's mind. Carrie looked at him. Really looked at him.

He met her eyes.

'But…I don't know who you are,' she said, in a low, strained voice. 'You could be anyone.'

Alexeis had never been told he 'could be anyone' before. The novelty intrigued him. But then the entire novelty of what he'd just done—what he was still doing and what he fully intended to do—was intriguing him. It was an experience he'd never had, and it had charms he had not anticipated. His identity had never been in question before.

Yet he could understand her caution and be pleased for it—for it only helped to recommend her to him. Half of his mind was telling him he was behaving with a rashness he would inevitably regret. The other half was determined to continue on the path his impulsiveness had started. After all, what real risk was there? There was nothing about the girl that was off-putting. Just the reverse. His original opinion of her had not changed—she was, indeed, very, very lovely.

So why not indulge his inexplicable whim and continue the evening with her? Besides, there had been something else that had made him so impulsively order his driver to stop. It was something to do with the way she had been walking— rapidly, but hunched up, head bowed. She'd looked— dejected. Down.

Clearly she needed something to divert her. Take her mind off her woes. So the whim he was following would be good for her, too, he reasoned. He would expect nothing of her she did not wish, and he would relinquish her at any point in the proceedings. But it would be a pity to do so now, so soon. Time to set her mind at rest. She was right, after all, to be cautious. Cities such as London could be dangerous for vul- nerable and beautiful young women.

He slipped a hand inside his inner breast pocket and drew out a slim silver card case, flicking it open and offering her a card from within.

'This will reassure you, I trust,' he said.

She took the card and looked at it.

'Alexe-is Ni-Nicol-ai-des,' she read, hesitating over the foreign syllables.

'You may have heard of the Nicolaides Group of compa- nies?' said Alexeis, a hint of arrogance in his voice.

The girl shook her head.

The sense of novelty struck Alexeis again. He had never encountered anyone who had not heard the name of Nicolaides. But then, of course, he moved in circles where everyone knew who had money and what that money derived from. Why should he expect a simple waitress to know such things?

'It is listed on several stock exchanges, and is capitalised at just under a billion euros. I am the chief executive, and my father the chairman. So you can see, I am sure, that I am quite respectable, and that you are, accordingly, perfectly safe.'

Carrie looked at Alexeis Nicolaides. The surname was a mouthful, but his first name seemed to quiver inside her, as if a vibration had been struck, very deep in her body. There was an uncertain expression on her face.

She ought to go. She ought to ask him to stop the car and let her out. So that she could walk briskly away. Back to her poky bedsit in the run-down house where she didn't know anyone, to eat toasted cheese for supper as she always did.

The prospect seemed bleak, uninviting, and into her mind crept another thought.

Would it be so very wrong to have dinner with him? This Alexeis Nicolaides, or whatever his name is. Do you think drinking champagne in a luxury car with a man who's obviously a millionaire and then having dinner with him is going to happen twice in your life? Do you?

But it wasn't his obvious wealth, or the luxury car and the brimming flutes of champagne that tempted her.

It was the man. The man who had made her breath catch when she'd first set eyes on him. The man she'd been unable not to stare at, to register as the most amazing-looking creature she'd ever seen.

She could feel part of her brain cut out. The part that was sensible and cautious. And sane.

Another part seemed to be pushing its way forward. Telling her something. Something that was getting more insistent. More persuasive.

More tempting to listen to.

Why not? Honestly, why not? You don't exactly have a packed social life, do you? You don't exactly have a million

people you know in London to go and see. You don't exactly
have anything else desperately urgent to do this evening, do
you? So why not? Why not? What have you got to lose?

'So,' Alexeis said, interrupting her thoughts. His voice
was still smooth, and again made her feel strange and fluttery
inside. 'You will have dinner with me?'

The expression of uncertainty deepened in her eyes.

'Um…' she said. 'I…I don't know. I…I…' She fell silent,
just staring at him helplessly, as if she was waiting for him
to make the decision for her.

He did. 'Good,' he said. 'Then that is settled. All we need
decide now is where you would like to eat. Would you like
to choose somewhere?'

He was, he knew, offering her the choice in order to make
her feel more in control of a situation that was overwhelming
her.

The look of uncertainty in her eyes deepened yet more.

'I…I don't really know anywhere in London,' she said.

He smiled. 'Fortunately, I do.'

Carrie made no answer. She couldn't. His smile had come
out of nowhere, and it electrified her. Dazzled her. Then it was
gone, leaving her nerves tingling. Alexeis took another
mouthful of champagne, and the movement triggered her to
do so as well.

'So, you have the advantage of my name, but not I of
yours,' he said encouragingly.

'It's Carrie—Carrie Richards,' she answered, almost
hesitantly.

Was she reluctant to give him her name? The novelty again
intrigued Alexeis, as did the faint colouring of her cheeks.
Women were usually eager for him to know who they were,
glad to draw his attention…

'Carrie,' he echoed. He lifted his glass in a toast. 'Well,

Carrie, I am enchanted to make your acquaintance,' he said, with a smile.

She bit her lip, still in a daze about the whole adventure, not seeing the way her gesture made his eyes focus on her mouth. She took another swallow of her champagne, feeling it fizzing warmly down her throat. It seemed to have fizzed into her veins as well. Suddenly she felt buoyant, as if everything were getting light around her. The dejected anxiety and depression she'd felt about losing her job, the bleak loneliness of living in London, seemed far away now, and she was glad and grateful. Grateful to the man who had dispelled it.

'Where are we going?' she asked, suddenly thrilled at the prospect.

'My hotel is by the river, and it has a very good restaurant, with a three-starred Michelin chef,' said Alexeis.

A look of sudden dismay crossed Carrie's face.

'Oh, I can't! I can't go into a restaurant—I've just realised! I mean—I'm still wearing this stupid uniform, and I haven't got any proper clothes with me!'

Alexeis gave a dismissive wave of his hand. 'That won't be a problem. Trust me.'

He smiled at her again. In the dim interior light, just for a moment, she felt a stab of unease go through her. Not just uncertainty. His smile had seemed, just for a moment, to be amusement at some private source of humour. Then he was speaking to her again, and the moment passed.

'Have you always lived in London?'

She shook her head. 'No, I've only been here a few months.'

'It must seem very exciting to you.' It was the sort of thing that seemed appropriate to say to a girl as beautiful as she was, at the peak of her youth.

But she gave a quick shake of her head again. 'No, I hate it!'

He looked taken aback. 'Why?'

'Everyone is so rude and unfriendly, and in a rush, pushing all the time.'

'Then why do you stay here?'

She gave an awkward half-shrug. 'It's where the work is.'

'There are no waitresses in your home town?'

She looked as though she were about to say something, then stopped herself. Alexeis wished he hadn't said what he had, lest she think it sarcastic. He hadn't meant it to be—he was simply surprised that a girl as beautiful as her had expressed so strong a dislike of London. She must have men flocking around her, and she could take her pick from them!

Even as the image formed in his mind he felt himself react. What he was doing was on impulse, he knew, but even with that allowance he still recognised his reaction. He didn't *want* her taking her pick of other men. Then his hackles retracted. While she was with him she would have eyes for no one else.

And nor would he...

There was no doubt in his mind about that, at any rate.

He let his gaze wash over her. She really did have something. He wasn't sure what, but it was growing on him with every passing moment.

'So where *is* your home town?' he asked, returning to the conversation. She was still uncertain about what she was doing, he could tell—and, again, the novelty of that uncertainty intrigued him. He knew of no women who had ever been in the least bit uncertain about their reaction if he showed the slightest interest. They positively bit his hand off when he took them up! They didn't bite their lip in that incredibly softly sensual way...

Another reaction took him, and he had to subdue it. It was far, far too soon for that! Now was only the time for gentling, for drawing her to him, for making her feel at ease—making her lose that last vestige of caution that would only encumber his plans for the evening.

'Um—it's Marchester,' she said. 'It's a small town, sort of in the Midlands.'

Alexeis had barely heard of it, and was little interested, but he made some anodyne reply, and continued the conversation with bare attention. He was far more interested in watching how a strand of her blonde hair had worked loose and was caressing her cheek, how her profile was etched against the windowpane. He was also impatient to arrive at the hotel and get her opposite him at a dining table, in a good light. Indulge himself in appreciating her soft beauty.

The car seemed to crawl the rest of the way, but eventually it drew up under the portico of the hotel—one of London's most prestigious, with breathtaking views over the Embankment.

As the driver opened his door, Alexeis crossed around the back of the car and helped her out, holding his hand to her. She took it tentatively, and it added, yet again, to her novelty value. Then his eyes were on the slender length of her black-stockinged leg, below the hem of her raincoat. She seemed to hug it more tightly around her as he escorted her into the hotel. She glanced around almost nervously.

'Don't worry—I won't subject you to a crowded restaurant,' he assured her. 'There is a much quieter place to eat upstairs.'

He guided her towards the bank of elevators, and in a moment they were being whisked upstairs. She had gone back to biting her lip again, he noticed.

Suddenly a pang struck him. Should he really be doing this?

Then she looked across at him and gave him a tentative smile, as if seeking reassurance. Something kicked through him, and his own uncertainty vanished. Her smile was enchanting—

He found himself smiling back at her. Giving her the reassurance she was silently seeking.

'It will be all right,' he said. 'I promise you.'

The flicker was in her eyes again. 'It's just that…just that…'

'It's just that I'm a complete stranger and I picked you up off the street.'

The blunt way he said it made her cheeks colour. But he had done it deliberately, spelling out her fears, her apprehension and unease.

'But think about this,' he went on, and his eyes held hers. 'The Irish have a saying—"All friends were strangers to each other once." Is that not true? We were not formally introduced to each other by mutual acquaintances—but so what? If I'd met you at a party I'd still have wanted to invite you to dinner. What difference does it make how we got to know each other?' His voice changed, something in his eyes changed, and something inside her shimmered and caught, like a soft flame lit deep, deep in her being. 'Now we do know each other. And over dinner, I trust, we will get to know each other more. But nothing, absolutely nothing, will happen that you do not want to happen. You have my word on this.'

His eyes held hers, and then, out of the solemnity, a smile slanted suddenly across his face. Carrie felt that dazzle glitter inside her, as it had done when she'd first seen that incredible smile in the car.

Slowly, she nodded, swallowing. She wasn't being stupid—she wasn't! She was simply being—

Carried away. Swept away. But why not? *Why not?* What was the harm in it? It was true, if she'd met him at a party she would not have been so nervous, so uneasy. And how could she walk away now? She didn't have the strength of

mind to do so. And she didn't have the will. Why should she?
He wasn't some seedy, creepy bloke—he was…gorgeous.
Fantastic. Devastating. Irresistible.

And someone like that would never appear twice in her
life.

The elevator doors opened and she stepped out.

Champagne still seemed to be fizzing in her veins.

CHAPTER THREE

THE 'somewhere quieter' that Alexeis had promised was quieter indeed. It was the dining room of his suite, overlooking the gardens of the Embankment below, and the dark, flowing Thames beyond. Her eyes had widened when she'd seen the view, but she had not objected or said anything, simply stared out over the river and the shore beyond.

'The Festival Hall, the National Theatre, the Hayward Gallery—all the South Bank,' said Alexeis, coming up behind her. His hand rested lightly and very casually on her shoulder as he pointed them out with his other hand. She felt warm beneath his touch, through the thin material of her blouse. She was like a gazelle, easily startled—easily affrighted—and so he kept his contact brief.

He stepped away, feeling a wry smile tugging at his mouth as his eyes flickered over her rear view. She had called her uniform 'stupid'. He had another word for it. But it was not one he would use in front of her. Instead, he would merely—enjoy it.

As, indeed, he proceeded to enjoy her company over dinner. He set himself out to dissolve her self-consciousness, her doubt about what she was doing here with him. He ventured several conventional opening gambits, such as

London's cultural life, but she said, looking rather awkward, that she did not go to the theatre and didn't know much about art. Immediately the memory of Marissa and her spouting self-importantly about the art world impinged in his mind, and he realised it was refreshing not to have to discuss such subjects. Whatever it was they did talk about—nothing too demanding or intellectual—he was very conscious of not being bored in any way. He was also conscious that he wanted her to feel comfortable and at ease.

And above all responsive to him.

But he was not overt. For her that would have been crass. This was not a female to come on strong to. This was one to…woo. A flicker came in his brain. Had that been the word he'd intended? Yes—and it was the right one, too. *Nothing will happen that she doesn't want,* he reminded himself.

Beneath the undemanding topics of conversation he was selecting for her benefit—tourist attractions in London was the current one—he considered her objectively. She must be in her mid-twenties, at least, and though she was reserved, it was a quality he liked about her. She would not have had appeal for him had she been otherwise. Nor, at that age, was it likely she was a virgin. Again, had she been, he would not have been in the slightest bit comfortable about what he was doing. But as it was—

She's here of her own volition, and I've all but spelt out to her that she only has to say the word and I will send her home untouched! I intend no harm to her—none whatsoever! Only a night we will both enjoy…

With final resolution, he closed his mind down on the matter. He was here to enjoy the evening—and, even more, the night ahead, he hoped. He wanted to ensure, as he was certain he was more than capable of doing, that she, too, took as much enjoyment as he did.

Satisfied with his conscience, he poured them both more champagne.

The meal was leisurely, superbly cooked and presented, and highly enjoyable. When, finally, it was over, Alexeis dismissed the waiting staff and guided her to the sofa for coffee, making sure he sat at the far end from her. He did not want her getting nerves at this stage.

His eyes rested on her.

He wanted her. It was very simple. Very uncomplicated. She was a beautiful female of a type he had never before encountered—a complete antidote to the kind of self-assured, self-regarding, sharply sophisticated women that were his usual fare. And he was intrigued by the prospect of what it would be like to experience her.

He was already diverted by the difference in his approach to her from his usual style. He had to be careful, he knew, not to appear to patronise her. She obviously had no experience of the kind of lifestyle he took for granted, and he wanted her to find enjoyment in the occasion. It was as if he wanted to—to indulge her.

It was an odd thought. He did not usually indulge the women he selected for his bed—if he had, they would have taken ruthless advantage of it. But this girl? No. Instinctively he knew that she would not do so.

Yet again, the novelty that she presented intrigued him.

He watched, his long lashes swept down over his dark eyes, as she nibbled from a rich chocolate truffle served on a silver filigree dish.

'I shouldn't, I know,' she said, a half-smile tugging at her mouth. She was not quite looking at him, as she had not quite looked at him all evening. 'But I can't resist.'

Alexeis smiled, stretching his arm out along the back of the sofa, but making sure it did not impinge into her body space. His eyes washed over her—the clinging blouse, the white apron, the tight skirt and the black stockings. The effect was erotic, yet very subtly so. He felt desire rise in him, and anticipation.

'Then don't,' he answered. 'Don't resist.'

Her eyes fluttered—and satisfaction eased in him. Oh, she might be unaware of how alluring she looked, but she was not unaware of her own response to him. Or of what it was that was happening between them.

And that was exactly what he wanted.

She finished the truffle—supremely conscious, he could see, of his regard—and then reached for her coffee. He did likewise, his eyes going to the hemline of her skirt, riding up over her knees. He felt his arousal quicken. But he must hasten slowly, he knew—draw her to him with extreme care—or he would frighten her off. Again the novelty of having to do so intrigued him.

As she sipped her coffee, he could see that she was becoming nervous, uneasy. There was an abstracted, unfocussed air about her. Then, as she finished the cup, she set it down on the coffee table and got to her feet. Alexeis's eyes followed the movement.

She stood, looking down at him.

'I ought to go,' she said. There was constriction in her voice. Agitation in the way she stood. 'I ought to go,' she said again.

Alexeis simply looked up at her, his pose still as relaxed as ever.

'Do you want to?' he asked.

She looked down at him, the soft fronds of her hair framing her face, the blackness of her stockings and the tightness of her skirt emphasising the slender length of her leg. He could see the swell of her breasts through the tight whiteness of her blouse.

He had not the least intention of letting her leave.

Of letting her *want* to leave.

She didn't speak, only looked at him. With indecision in her eyes, colour in her cheeks. He set down his coffee cup, but otherwise did not move.

'I would like you very much to stay,' he said.

She bit her lip. Alexeis got to his feet and came up to her. She did not move.

His eyes rested on her.

'I promised you,' he said in a low voice, 'that I would at any time call the car to drive you home. That is as true now as it was then. And if you wish it I shall do so. But...' His eyes rested on her with an intent he wanted her to feel. 'I would like, before I do so, to do one thing. This—'

He stepped forward. In a single fluid movement, before she could back away or realise what he was going to do, he slid his hands around the frame of her jaw, slid his fingers into the silken mass of her hair, cupping her head, tilting it to him, and then, closing up to her, he lowered his mouth down to hers.

She was as soft as honey, as warm and sweet. He parted her lips to taste the sweeter appeal within.

She made no resistance to him. None. With a tiny sigh, deep in her throat, she parted for him, letting him taste her, letting his tongue glide into her mouth, deepening his kiss so that as the tender swell of her breasts brushed against him he could feel, with a deep, sensual satisfaction, their tips harden.

Ruthlessly, he increased the sensuality of his kiss, one hand slipping from her jaw to glide with sensuous leisure down the supple length of her spine, drawing her yet closer against him. Curving down over the rounded swell of her bottom so barely covered by the enticing tightness of her skirt.

As he drew her against him, his stance altering instinctively to accommodate her body against the cradle of his hips, he felt her give a soft gasp. It aroused him yet further, and he let his hand edge further down, seeking the hemline of her skirt and ruching it upwards, so that his hand splayed over only the barest, sheerest material between it and her naked flesh.

God, but she was lovely to kiss, to caress. Her sweet, enticing body yielding to his, moulding to his, her tender mouth open to his to taste at will—

Desire speared in him—strong, aroused. Insistent.

He dragged his mouth from hers, still holding her against him. From somewhere, somewhere that required all his strength, he found his voice.

'Do you still want to leave, Carrie?'

She was staring at him blindly, her pupils huge, lips parted. He could see the hectic pulse at her throat, feel the agitation of her heart against his chest, the peaked tips of her breasts.

She made no answer.

With triumph surging through him, he lowered his mouth to hers again.

Carrie lay, curled back against Alexeis's strong, hard body. Her mind felt overwhelmed, her body still glowing, pulsing, with what she had experienced.

Which had been something even the most fervid imagination could never, never have imagined!

Oh, God, it had been incredible—amazing! Unbelievable!

Disbelief, wonder, seared through her.

I never knew it could be like that! Never!

She had not stood a chance, she knew—not a single chance of changing her mind. Not from the moment when, filled with the sudden inescapable realisation of why she had come here, she had suddenly felt that she was far, far out of her depth. All the temptation of the evening had suddenly coalesced into reality. The reality of what she was allowing to happen.

Why not? The voice had said to her again.

But at that fateful moment last night, looking down at the superb, lounging figure of the man who had simply knocked the breath from her body the first time she'd set eyes on him, the only words in her mind had been quite, quite different.

Oh, my God—what am I doing—what am I doing?

But she had known—known absolutely—what she was doing. Had known it all evening and had gone with it. Gone with the voice that had tempted her.

And she had known in that moment of standing there, at the end of the evening, that the moment of decision had come. She had known why she was there—known exactly why. There had been only one decision to be made—did she want to stay? To accept what was going to happen? To succumb to the temptation that had been beckoning her all evening?

She stared ahead of her, out over the dimness of the bedroom. What might she have answered had Alexeis not kissed her?

She didn't know. Because he *had* kissed her, and in that very first moment, when his cool, long fingers had slid into her hair and his mouth had come down on hers, there had been only one decision—and it had already been made.

And she could not—did not—regret it! Not now, as she lay there, scooped back against the fantastic body that had done things to hers that she had never known were possible! How could she possibly regret it?

It had been a feast of sensuality—a banquet! His touch on her had melted through her like lava, drawing from her a response she had not thought possible. Touch after touch, each more arousing than the last, each more devastatingly intimate, until at last the sensations in her body, so incredible, so exquisite, had fused into an endless stream, intensifying until she was molten. Helpless in his arms, her head threshing from side to side, her body had been incandescent, burning like a flame that consumed all sense, all knowledge, all consciousness, making the whole world only what she was feeling, as if the whole universe were inside her head and nothing else existed!

Only the man making her feel that way. Only the one she'd clung to, cried out to, clutched with her hands, lifted her body to, to catch more, yet more, of that incredible, incredible experience—

She felt the afterglow still infusing through her, in her flesh. Her eyes were heavy, lids sinking. Her lashes fluttered. Around her waist she could feel, like a band, his strong arm pinioning her to him. Holding her where he wanted her to be.

In his arms. His bed.

CHAPTER FOUR

CARRIE sat in the wide leather seat in the first-class compartment of the aeroplane, overcome with wonder and disbelief.

What on earth am I doing? What on earth am I doing?

The words circled slowly in her brain. It was hard to think coherently, rationally. Hard to think at all. She didn't want to, she knew. She wanted very much not to think. To simply— accept. Accept that something had happened that had never happened to her in her life before and never would again. She had spent the night—the most amazing, incredible, breathtaking night of her life!—with a man who had been a stranger twenty-four hours ago. And now, even more unbelievably, she was flying to New York with him!

It was like some kind of fantasy—the kind you dreamt up when life looked grim and you needed something rose-tinted and impossibly wonderful to think about. The mental equivalent of eating a cream cake or pigging out on a box of Belgian chocolates.

Her head turned to look at the most incredible man in the world, sitting beside her—an entire tray of cream cakes, a kilo of Belgian chocolates all in his own right!

She gazed helplessly, disbelievingly, at his profile. His attention was focussed on the screen of his laptop, resting on the table provided by the airline seat, his long legs extended.

Her heart swelled. God, he was so gorgeous to look at! She could gaze at him non-stop, like an idiot, just drinking him in. Everything about him was incredible—from the strong nape of his neck, the dark satin sheen of his superbly cut hair to the strong line of his jaw, the sweep of lashes around those eyes that could melt, melt, *melt* her into mush just by glancing at her...

A thrill went through her like a huge bubble of champagne, lifting her from her seat.

I'm with him—I'm really with him! He's taking me to New York and I can go on being with him all that time!

That was the thought she wanted to go on thinking—feeling—like champagne in her veins, intoxicating her. But the other thought—the one that was trying to circle slowly—was also there.

What am I doing here?

The only answer she could give was the wonder, disbelief and delight that was intoxicating her. That was all the answer there was.

I'm here because I couldn't be otherwise! I couldn't turn it down—couldn't say no. How could I have? How could I have?

In less than twenty-four hours her life had been turned upside down and she had been swept away. And she was helpless, quite helpless, to do anything else but let it happen.

A deep, heartfelt sigh of sheer happiness breathed from her.

Beside her, Alexeis, supremely conscious of the slender, beautiful body so close to his, heard her exhalation and glanced at her. Approval and satisfaction reflected in his eyes before he turned back to his work.

Yes, he had made a good decision. Definitely a good decision. A good decision to follow the unexpected impulse that had impelled him to order the car to stop as it drove past her, and a good decision to fold her soft, yielding body to his and make her his own. It had been an amazing night. Extraordinary not just for the novelty of it but for whatever it was that had made possessing her so deeply satisfying. He wanted—quite naturally, quite obviously—to repeat the experience for quite some time, he knew, and to do that he'd needed to make the decision he had made this morning: to take Carrie with him. Yes, it was an impulse. No, he did not normally take women with him. But so what? He was taking Carrie with him. Why? Because she was, right now, exactly what he wanted.

Rapidly, mentally, he ran through just why that was. She was beautiful, obviously—he wouldn't have bothered with her otherwise. But hers was a beauty, a wide-eyed, fair-haired, tender-mouthed loveliness—that appealed to a taste in him that he hadn't hitherto been aware of. That in itself was a charm that he was more than appreciative of. Her body was all that he could want—soft breasts, slender waist, gently rounded hips, long legs, and skin like the satin bloom of a peach growing into ripeness.

Caressing her, possessing her, had been a pleasure that was as rewarding as he had anticipated.

A slight frown flickered in his eyes. She had been everything he'd expected, it was true—soft, silken, and very, very seducible. And she hadn't been, as he had known, a virgin. That, he knew, he would have found an impediment. However, she was not much experienced—certainly not in all the ways of pleasure he was used to. He had sensed her inexperience in some forms of intimacy, had sensed, too—a sensual smile of recollection played about his mouth as memory caressed his mind—how much of a revelation it had been to her that such intensity of sensation was possible…

She had gasped, cried out, eyes distended, wonder and amazement in her face, as he had brought her time after time to the point of ecstasy. It had been, he mused, a particular satisfaction of his own to afford her such an experience as she had clearly never known before.

The frown flickered in his eyes again. It was a novelty, he knew, to have a sexual partner such as she was—one he had to lead almost every step of the way. And his reward had been more than pleasure. Something had made him want to watch, intently, as her body caught fire from his ministrations, to hear her cry out, and then, as the fire ebbed from her, the flames of ecstasy extinguished, to fold her to him, to hold her, cradle her. Then, as he had reaped his own reward, his own rich satiation, something more had made him feel that it was a feeling richer than any he had felt with any other woman…

But why not? he reasoned. She was not like his usual fare, so his experience, his response, had been different. That was all. Simply—different.

He turned to glance at her again. She was leafing through a glossy magazine now—her head slightly bowed and her lovely profile exposed to him—and he let his eyes linger a moment. Yes, different indeed. And not just in looks and style.

In personality too.

She was quiet, for a start. She did not try to talk to him, to make sophisticated conversation or demands of him. She simply gave a fleeting smile, almost shy, her eyes only briefly meeting his, before drawing away as if she were not sure whether to look at him. Nor did she seem, like all the other women of his acquaintance, to relish and revel in the attentions of other men. All the women he had selected for his leisure hours had always known how prized they were, and had taken it for granted—expected it as their due—that male eyes would be drawn to them.

Carrie was not like that. She seemed rather to be embarrassed by heads turning as she walked beside him. Alexeis had been highly aware of how she had immediately drawn male attention when she came into the airport, and when they boarded the plane. But she had seemed either unconscious of the way men were looking at her or, at the other extreme, uncomfortable with it.

He had never known a woman with her calibre of looks to be so.

He had put it down to her being self-conscious about her new clothes. She had spent the day in Knightsbridge, with a personal shopper that his London PA had organised, and when she had walked into the VIP lounge he had known at once that it had been well worthwhile.

If she had looked unknowingly erotic in that black and white uniform last night, now she simply looked stunning. She was wearing a pale aqua suit, with bracelet-length jacket sleeves and a pencil skirt, and her hair was dressed in a style that was simple, but extremely effective, the front strands drawn back to the nape of her neck to give her a profile that was almost pre-Raphaelite.

He had not been able to take his eyes from her.

As he'd escorted her on to the plane he'd known, with absolute certainty, that he had definitely—quite definitely—made an excellent decision.

Two weeks in New York. Two weeks with Alexeis. Two weeks of a world, a life, Carrie had never dreamt of having. Far, far different from anything she had ever known. With every day—more with every night—her real life seemed a universe away. With every day this new life she was leading was becoming more and more real to her.

And yet still a fantasy come true.

How could it not be? How could it not be like a fantasy to be staying in a world-famous hotel by Central Park, a guest in a lavishly appointed suite, eating in one gourmet restaurant after another, dressed in clothes that she had only ever before seen in glossy magazines. Night after night to be taken to glamorous, glittering parties, sometimes in fantastic multi-storeyed apartments in uptown Manhattan, sometimes in the mansions of Long Island, drinking champagne as if it were water, wearing evening gowns so beautiful they were fit for a princess. How could it not be a fantasy come true?

And to have at the glowing, radiant heart of it Alexeis at her side.

Just thinking about him made her weak with longing for him. The hours without him seemed endless, and though she knew, of course, that he was here on business, she had to school herself to patience until she could be with him again—even if much of the time it was in public rather than in private. He socialised a great deal, but he didn't seem to mind that she was a less than scintillating partner for him. All of the women they'd met in New York seemed to have high-powered careers, or else be engrossed in a host of other activities—running charity events, involved in the arts or media or fashion—always something glamorous, something prestigious, something that made Carrie feel dull and boring in comparison.

But she wouldn't let it get her down. After all, she would remind herself, if Alexeis didn't mind her being so different from the glamorously sophisticated circles he moved in, then why should she? And besides, when she was alone with Alexeis she didn't feel dull or awkward. Even though he lived in so utterly a different world from her, came from so entirely a different background, it didn't seem to matter. Being with him, she just felt—at ease.

She didn't know why—didn't question it. Only accepted it—gratefully. Just as she accepted that he had, for reasons she did not question either, swept her away into this wonderful, wonderful world with him.

Nor did she ask the question she dreaded—how long would she have with him? How long before the fantasy ended and Alexeis left her life as swiftly as he had entered it?

But she wouldn't think about that. Hurriedly she pulled her mind away. She would make the most, the very most, of each and every wonderful day—and more, the passionate, breathtaking nights she had with him, living out this most incredible of romantic fantasies…

For as she knew this could only *be* a fantasy, she also knew, with a strange tremor of her heart, that there could never, ever again be a man in her life like Alexeis. It was not just the wealth and the glamour—that was only the gilding. The gold—the pure, pure gold—was Alexeis himself. He was her treasure, who made this time so precious.

And when it ended…?

No—again she pushed the thought aside. It would come, but not yet. Not yet. Not today—not tonight.

But come it did. When Alexeis's final day in New York arrived, Carrie was still determined not to think of it. Yet it seemed that there was a hard, heavy stone inside her chest. At breakfast she was subdued, picking at her food.

'You are not hungry?' Alexeis eyebrows rose in surprise. Carrie always ate heartily in the morning—but then, like him, she needed to restore her energy levels after the exertions of the night.

'No, not really,' she answered, and set down her fork, abandoning half of the delicious Eggs Benedict that she usually polished off. But she had no appetite—only that hard, heavy stone inside her.

'You don't feel well?' he asked. There was concern in his voice.

She gave a quick shake of her head. 'It's just because it's the last day,' she said.

'So New York has enraptured you?' he commented. 'Even though—' a note of mock severity came into his voice '—you have hardly made the most of all the shops! Well, perhaps those in Chicago will tempt you more, *ne*?'

'Chicago?' Carrie's voice was puzzled.

'Our next destination,' said Alexeis. He looked at her. 'You have no urgent need to go back to London, do you?'

Carrie stared at him. The hard, heavy stone inside her seemed to be poised on the brink of melting away like snow in summer. But did she dare believe what he might be saying?

Alexeis watched her expression. It was something he found very enjoyable to do—and not just now. He had enjoyed watching her expression on their first evening in New York, when she'd gazed at her reflection, wearing an evening gown that had cost five thousand dollars. Her face had come alight with disbelief and wonder at the image she had made. And when he'd escorted her to cocktails on the rooftop terrace of a skyscraper, or to a party on a multi-million-dollar yacht on the Hudson, to dress circle seats at the latest Broadway musical. Wherever he took her, whatever the experience, the location, her face was so very, very expressive.

And not just as she was experiencing what life was like when she was at his side. What he enjoyed most of all was watching her face as he made love to her. He took almost as much pleasure in her pleasure, as he took in his own.

And he took pleasure, too, in just being with her. That was strange for him, he knew. With other women, their primary value to him was as a sexual partner, skilled and experienced.

Sophisticated in their tastes and expertise, they were social partners too, who could be relied on to move easily in his world. But not otherwise to spend time with. But Carrie—well, she was different. She seemed just to—to be there—part of his daily life.

He frowned minutely. He'd never thought of women in that way—as companions. His frown deepened. When he was alone with Carrie, what did they do? What did they talk about? He tried to think. Obviously a great deal of their time together they were in bed, but, even so, there was a lot of time when he was not making love to her. When he was simply having breakfast with her, chatting, relaxed, or late at night or in the early morning, together in bed, embracing her, half asleep, half awake, talking of... Well, what *did* they talk about? Nothing specific, nothing memorable. Yet the very fact that he could not recall was in itself notable.

The more so because he had had to accept Carrie was not the kind of person who could hold her own in the subjects for social discourse that he typically took for granted. She did not opine volubly on subjects such as politics or economics, culture or fashion. She did not opine volubly on anything—she kept to his side, quiet, unobtrusive, almost shy. Yet with him alone she was not subdued, not restrained. So the question formed in his mind again. What did they talk about? Unexceptional, easy, undemanding things.

Trivial things? No—that was the wrong word. Belittling. It didn't suit her. So what word *did*?

Sweet-natured. That was the word that came to him when he thought of Carrie. The frown came again. He realised that he thought about her more than he usually thought about any woman. With other women it was out of sight, out of mind—unless he was in the mood for sex. But with Carrie—well, he found himself thinking about her even in the middle of a demanding business meeting, or when his head was full of financial figures. And not just because he wanted to get back to the hotel suite and whisk her off to bed! No, he found himself thinking of the way she smiled, the way she gazed at him, the way she frowned slightly when she asked him some question about, say, a sight she'd seen that day, or someone she'd met the evening before.

He paused. That was another thing. They might be travelling back from a party, talking about the evening and who had been there, and she would come out with comments about their hosts, or other guests, that were all the more perceptive for her not knowing them well. Perhaps her perceptiveness came from the fact that she was quiet, that she tended to observe, not participate? Almost—he smiled to himself at the metaphor—as if she were studying people through a microscope, watching attentively, reading their reactions to each other. But not interacting with them herself. Keeping herself a little apart.

But not from him. The sense of satisfaction he always felt when he thought about Carrie, about his decision to take her with him, resonated through him. No, Carrie did not keep herself apart from him—the very opposite! There was no veiling of her reaction to him—just as now there was no veiling of the shining happiness clearly radiant in her eyes because he had no intention, *absolutely* no intention, of ending their relationship.

'So…' He leant back, his eyes resting warmly on her expressive face. 'I take it that's a yes for Chicago?'

She didn't need to say anything to give him the answer he wanted. But he saw that it was with renewed vigour that she resumed tucking into her breakfast.

CHAPTER FIVE

BEING in Chicago with Alexeis was just as wonderful as being in New York. As was San Francisco, and then Atlanta, and then, after America, back across the Atlantic in Milan. Being anywhere with him was wonderful—anywhere at all!

For as long as he wanted her.

And he did seem to want her! That was the amazing, fantastical thing! She had given up wondering at it, worrying about it. Time seemed to have stopped. Past and future seemed to have slipped away—there was only an endless, wonderful 'now' that swept her away on wings of wonder and delight. A 'now' that was focussed only and entirely on Alexeis.

Alexeis. Irresistible Alexeis. Carrie was helpless and could only give herself to him—time after time, night after night. His care of her, his consideration, the way he laughed and met her eyes with wry amusement, the way she felt at ease with him, chatting about…well, she wasn't sure what. But it all came easily, and she didn't feel awkward or shy in his company, however intimidated she sometimes felt when she was out in public with him. She knew his sophisticated friends and acquaintances must think her dull, but she was used to that, and Alexeis didn't seem to mind one bit.

Sometimes when she thought about it—and she tried not to—it seemed amazing to her that a man so worldly and sophisticated as Alexeis Nicolaides should actually want to spend time with her. His personality was so strong, so vibrant—surely he should want a woman to match? Not to mention, she thought with a little worried catch of her breath, a woman who could move in his world with confidence and assurance.

Yet still he kept her with him, still he showed no sign of getting bored or tired of her—and how could she possibly bring herself to question that? With yet another catch of breath, a tightening of her lungs, she wondered how she could possibly ever want this to end.

But as they ascended in the lift to Alexeis's suite in the five-star hotel in Milan, Carrie couldn't help wishing his lifestyle were not quite so unsettled. At first the thrill of visiting foreign places, staying in luxury hotels, had widened her eyes in wonder. But now, after weeks of long, tiring flights and living out of suitcases—albeit crammed with exquisite clothes!—she found herself longing simply to stay put somewhere.

Guilt speared her even as she thought it, and she felt wretchedly ungrateful, but she still couldn't help saying impulsively, 'Do you always travel so much?'

He cast a glance at her. 'There are Nicolaides companies on three continents—I like to keep tabs on them,' he said. Then his expression changed. 'Are you getting tired of globe-trotting?' There was a sympathetic note in his voice, and Carrie smiled apologetically.

'Do I sound like a graceless brat?' she said ruefully. 'You've taken me to places I'd never, ever have had a chance of seeing!'

He slipped his hand into hers and she felt its warmth, its strength.

'Well, let me do what I must in Milan, and then—' his expression softened '—how about if we run away and have a holiday? The weather's warming up now, and I could do with some time off. Does that sound good?'

Her heart swelled. 'Blissful,' she sighed. 'Oh, Alexeis, you are so good to me!'

He lifted her hand to his mouth. 'And you, my sweet Carrie, are good for *me*.'

His lips brushed her knuckles softly. 'My first meeting isn't for over an hour. Tell me…' his eyes glinted in the way that made her knees weaken '…are you very jet-lagged, hmm?'

The flare of colour across her cheeks gave him all the answer he needed, and he cut it very fine indeed, getting to his meeting.

That evening, to add to her happiness, they dined alone in their suite, which they didn't do very often, and Carrie treasured the occasion.

'Tomorrow,' announced Alexeis, 'you must go shopping. You must take advantage of Milan being the fashion capital of the world.'

Immediately Carrie demurred. 'Oh, no. I have so many clothes already! I can't possibly need any more!'

A smile played around his well-shaped mouth. 'I've never known a woman so reluctant to let me adorn her!'

She bit her lip. 'I don't want you spending so much money on me, Alexeis,' she said, a touch of awkwardness in her voice.

He cast an indulgent look at her across the table. 'I have a lot to spend,' he said casually.

But her expression remained troubled. 'I know you work hard, Alexeis, but…' She paused. He raised an eyebrow. Hesitantly she went on, 'It's such a…a strange life,' she said slowly. 'Constant travelling, taking luxury for granted, spending so much all the time. Is that…is that all you want to do? All your life?'

As she spoke, she wished she hadn't. Who was she to question Alexeis's life when she was enjoying all the luxury he lavished on her?

There was an odd look in his eye as he answered, his fingers closing around the stem of a wine glass holding a vintage that she knew would probably have cost more than she could earn in a week.

'Do you think I should settle down?'

She swallowed. There was something in his voice that made her uneasy.

'It isn't what I think—it's none of my concern what you do with your life—but… Well, don't you ever *want* to settle down?'

His mouth twisted suddenly. 'It's what my mother would like!' he said.

'Your mother?' Carrie stared at him. It was impossible to think of Alexeis with a mother, a family. He was like some dark and dashing hero in a fantasy, sprung ready-made from the female imagination!

But Alexeis did not answer her. Instead, he refilled his glass. Why had he mentioned his mother? Was it because Carrie had brought up the subject of his constantly peripatetic life? A life he had adopted deliberately, he knew, because it took him away from the unrealistic expectations of his mother—and, even more, the unwelcome company of his father.

He raised the glass to his mouth and let his gaze rest on Carrie, a frown in his eyes. She had asked if he wanted to 'settle down'. Did that mean she was starting to get ideas? The kind of ideas that would only lead to the ending of her association with him? His mouth tightened. If it did mean that it was a nuisance! He had no desire whatsoever to replace her.

What he did want—and the realisation was suddenly very clear in his head—was to take her off somewhere he could be with her twenty-four hours a day, seven days a week, for a decent length of time. Somewhere the endless preoccupations of the Nicolaides Group would not need attending to. He'd mentioned taking her on holiday—and that was exactly what he wanted to do. His mind raced ahead. He would compact his time in Milan, and then, by the weekend, he should be free to leave. With luck, he might be able to squeeze a week's holiday away from work—possibly two, even.

There was another reason, too, why he would welcome being out of contact for a while. His Milanese PA had informed him that his mother had been in touch, and wanted him to phone as soon as possible. So far he had avoided it, telling his PA he was too tied up, because he knew he would immediately come under his mother's pressure to make a stop-over in Greece. And if he did that his mother would inevitably want him to socialise, and would start dangling potential brides in front of him, as she always did.

Exasperation bit through him. Why could she not accept that he had no intention of marrying—let alone for the reasons she wanted? He knew she was both venomous and paranoid about her ex-husband, but he was not into playing her power games. He would run the Nicolaides Group, giving his father the time off he wanted to indulge his sex-life, and paying him the least attention he could. He certainly would not resort to marrying an heiress, or delivering his father a grandson simply to carry on the dynasty!

It was time—more than time—for his mother to accept that, and to leave him in peace from her endless machinations.

Leave him to enjoy the life he led, working hard but with the pleasures of any woman he wanted for his purpose.

In his mind's eye he envisaged Carrie standing beside him on the moonlit deck of a yacht, his arm around her, her soft, warm body leaning against his, gazing out over the sea…

He brought his thoughts back to the present. In the meantime, he would enjoy taking her to La Scala tomorrow night—and enjoy even more seeing her in yet another exquisite evening gown.

'Tomorrow,' he announced, 'you must visit the Quadrilatero d'Oro—Milan's couture fashion quarter. Your mission will be to buy a gown suitable for the opera at the grandest of Italian opera houses.'

'Oh, but I have so many evening gowns already,' she said immediately.

He waved this consideration aside. 'I particularly want you to look your best,' he said. He did not explain why, but he had a pretty shrewd idea that Adrianna would know he was in Milan, and would be eager to see him. He wanted Carrie to give a clear message that she was the new incumbent, and that Adrianna was history.

Reluctant though she was to spend yet more money on clothes, nevertheless Carrie did as Alexeis asked—helped by the fact that she had fallen in love with an ankle-length narrow white evening gown, with shoestring straps and a softly draped bodice that didn't show her décolletage.

She dressed her hair in a low, loose chignon, and kept her make-up low key. It seemed to meet Alexeis's approval, and she was glad—especially when she had to admit that she knew nothing about Italian grand opera.

'Well, see what you make of it,' said Alexeis smoothly. 'It is an acquired taste.'

Would she take to it? he wondered. Despite being in Milan, she was not interested in fashion, nor in art either, saying she knew nothing about them. Nor did she seem to know about the history of the city or Italy itself, although she did show an interest when Alexeis enlightened her. He forbore to comment—it was not, after all, her fault if her education had been lacking. He had had the privilege of an extremely expensive education—whereas Carrie clearly had not. He could not blame her for her shortcomings. And did they matter, anyway, in the end?

Carrie might not be well-educated, but she was unfailingly polite and considerate, and courteous to everyone, with her shy smile and a placid temperament that seemed to come naturally to her. It made her, he knew, much easier to be with than other women. And whilst he was well aware that some of his acquaintances were more than ready to assume her prime attraction for him was her looks, he was unconcerned. What he got from Carrie was different from what he'd ever got from anyone else, and for the time being that was what he wanted.

And when, upon their arrival at the crowded opera house, Adrianna chose to sweep dramatically up to him, Alexeis saw no reason to change his mind. Voluptuous in dark red satin, her lush brunette locks glossy and richly coloured, rubies heaving on the swell of her exposed breasts, Adrianna launched into voluble Italian—a tirade of reproach and cajolement. Alexeis's face closed, and then he simply said, 'Adrianna,' in both acknowledgement and dismissal, and moved on, leaving her seething behind him.

At his side, he could feel that Carrie had stiffened, but she said nothing, and he was glad.

His hand tightened on Carrie's elbow, and he steered her upstairs to his private box, pausing to meet and greet his myriad acquaintance *en route*. He made no reference to Adrianna, or they to him about her, though he knew it would provide food for gossip. It was with a sense of relief that he closed the door of the box, and took his seat next to Carrie. She was studying the programme, her brow slightly furrowed.

'Do you know the story of *Madame Butterfly*?' he asked conversationally.

'Not really,' she answered, giving him a hesitant look. 'But it explains the plot here.' She indicated the programme notes.

'Well, I hope you will enjoy it,' Alexeis said smoothly.

Carrie's smile flickered uncertainly. Her thoughts were elsewhere—with the woman who had accosted Alexeis earlier. An old flame? Or someone who wanted to be a new flame? The woman had looked at her with open contempt, and Carrie had felt the sting of it even without understanding what she'd been saying. She had wanted to ask Alexeis, but he hadn't volunteered any information, so presumably he didn't want to talk about it.

She let it pass, instead gazing around at the splendour of the newly refurbished opera house, resplendent in crimson and gold, its horseshoe of boxes encircling the stage. Even though she knew nothing about Italian opera, she knew that being taken here by Alexeis, sitting beside him in a beautiful gown in his private box, would be a memory to treasure. The orchestra finished tuning up, the house lights started to dim, and the conductor took the podium. Carrie settled back, ready to enjoy the evening.

Except that she didn't. The music, yes, was rapturous, but as the opera progressed Carrie found herself disliking it more and more. Found it increasingly disturbing that poor, foolish Madame Butterfly seemed so completely besotted with a man for whom she was nothing more than a novelty—an impulsive indulgence to while away time in a foreign port, to be wooed and seduced with sweet words and smiles, but never to be taken seriously. Carrie's mood, when the tragic end inevitably came, was sombre, her thoughts unwelcome.

As the applause finally died away, and the audience started to move, Alexeis turned to her.

'So, did you enjoy it?' he asked. There was a look of expectation on his face.

Carrie bit her lip. 'Not really,' she said apologetically. It was all she could think of saying.

Alexeis's expression altered. 'Ah, well—as I say, it's an acquired taste, opera,' he allowed.

'I'm sorry,' said Carrie. She felt she had disappointed him. She wanted to say more, but didn't know how to say it without seeming critical and ungrateful of having been taken to such a glittering and glamorous event.

'Not at all,' Alexeis said smoothly. 'Perhaps it is too emotional for English tastes? Overwrought and melodramatic!'

Carrie smiled uncertainly as they made their way out of the box. 'Overwrought and melodramatic' was perhaps one way of describing the ending of *Madame Butterfly*, but to Carrie it had just seemed terrible. How could the heroine, however much she loved the faithless hero, possibly hand over their infant son to his wife to raise and then kill herself?

Emotion pierced her, borne on the echoing tide of the wrenching music still sounding in her head. Grief, pitiless and cruel, made her live again her own terrible, unbearable day, when her father had collected her from school, his face ashen, tears running down his cheeks. A car crash, a speeding lorry, and her mother dead for ever.

And then, more recent still, her father's death—fought against day after day, for three long, agonising years, until the final defeat had come.

She bowed her head, blinking. She must not think of that—what was the point? She must think only of the most important thing—that her father had achieved what he most wanted to achieve in life before he'd lost the battle.

And life—*her* life—had to go on. She knew that. It had been hard in material terms, punishingly so, but there had been no alternative.

Until that evening at the art gallery. When she had first set eyes on Alexeis—and he on her. That wonderful, unforgettable evening when he'd turned her life upside down and swept her off her feet. Her eyes shadowed suddenly. Just as Madame Butterfly had been swept off her feet…

But I'm not poor, deluded Madame Butterfly!

Yes, she had been swept off her feet by Alexeis—but where was the harm in that? Yes, it was like a fantasy come true—but what could possibly be wrong about being swept off her feet by a man as gorgeous and as wonderful as Alexeis? How could she resist the heavenly way he made her feel when he made love to her, the feelings and sensations she hadn't even known it was possible to have? The nights when he would turn to her, his long, dark lashes sweeping down over his eyes, their intent clear…so very, very clear? She shivered in recollection and anticipation.

Of course she was revelling in it, in this wonderful, amazing time she was having. With Alexeis wanting her, taking her everywhere with him! And of course it wasn't real and would not last—could not last. But while it did, while he still desired her, how could she possibly walk away from it?

What reason could she have for doing so?

Yet later that night, as she lay in the embracing cradle of Alexeis's arms, she heard again the soaring notes of the opera's music tearing at her. She gazed out into the darkness of the room. Around her she could feel Alexeis's arms, behind

her the strong wall of his chest. She might be living in a
fantasy, but the arms around her were real—so very real.

Disturbingly real.

Unease plucked at her heart.

Yet in the morning it was gone, banished in the bright
sunshine. Alexeis had left her with a warm kiss, and instructions to buy herself clothes suitable for a holiday.

'I'll be clear by the weekend and we'll fly down to Genoa,
where the yacht will be waiting for us.' He had smiled. 'Just
you and me.'

Her spirits had lifted instantly, and they had stayed lifted,
all troubling thoughts and feelings gone. And now she was
racing through the cobalt waters of the Mediterranean on a
luxury motor yacht, along the Ligurian coastline to the fashionable Italian resort of Positano. But best of all was having
Alexeis to herself, without any socialising, at ease together,
just the two of them.

It was Alexeis, not the luxury of his lifestyle, that capti-
vated her. Alexeis who turned her bones to water, whose
touch melted her like honey. Alexeis for whom she made
herself as beautiful as she could, in whose embrace she discovered, time after time, a bliss that overwhelmed her.

It did so yet again, while they were making love in the afternoon in the sun-drenched cabin, and the sunlight on the
water reflected all around them, while the world rocked
gently beneath her—an unforgettable experience.

She lifted a hand to his dark silken hair and gazed up at
him. She didn't say anything, her fingers sifting through his
hair as he looked down at her. There was a strange look in his
eye. She didn't know what it was, but it made her feel—different.

Alexeis was always appreciative of her—always made
time after sex to hold her a while, let her come down from the

heights he took her to, almost as if he enjoyed knowing that she had been there. He was patient with her, giving her time to be calm and let her hectic, throbbing heart-rate slow and ease again. It sometimes amazed her that he should be so attentive to her needs.

She had lost track of the passage of time, content simply to lie there, feeling the warm, intimate closeness of his body, saying nothing, just gazing up at him.

He looked down at her, his elbow resting on the pillow, propping up his head, still with that strange, unfamiliar light in his eye. He lifted a finger of his free hand and softly traced the outline of her lips. Then he gave a half-smile, as if to himself. He had been right to take Carrie away like this, have her to himself, with all the indulgence of being off duty, away from the demands of work. It was curious, he mused, that he still desired her so much, still enjoyed her so much. Was so content, still, to keep her with him.

His smile deepened as his eyes washed over her. She was gazing up at him with a soft, dreamy look on her face, her body warm beneath his, the pattern of sunlight dancing on the walls, the boat rocking lazily on the water. Alexeis went on smoothing her hair and looking down at her, eyelids half closing.

Right now there was nothing more he wanted. He wasn't going to question it, wasn't going to analyse it. He was just going to accept it. Enjoy it.

Contentment eased through him.

His mood of contentment lasted until dimly, through the haze of sleep that he had drifted into, Alexeis heard his phone ringing. He cursed silently. He'd given instructions only to be contacted in absolute necessity, and the last thing he wanted was his holiday interrupted with work. Even though it clicked to voicemail and went silent, a few moments later it started ringing again. Irritated, Alexeis unwound a now sleeping Carrie's arms from around him, and went to answer it. As he picked up his phone, it clicked again to voicemail, and he hit 'replay'.

It his mother, and his mood instantly worsened. As he listened, his expression steeled. Expletives sounded in his mind. Hell, this just *wasn't* what he needed.

His mother had found him another heiress.

She was a brand-new one—Anastasia Savarkos. Her brother, Leo, had just been disinherited by their grandfather, and Anastasia had been pronounced the sole Savarkos heiress—a rich prize indeed. A prize that his mother was determined her son should snap up before anyone else did.

To that end, her voicemail informed him, she had invited Anastasia at short notice to one of her regular summer house parties at her villa on the Ionian island of Lefkali—and she now summoned Alexeis there as well, for dinner the following night. No, thought Alexeis grimly, he would not attend! And if his mother had planted expectations in Anastasia Savarkos's head, then tough. He was *not* about to go running to Lefkali to indulge his mother's ludicrous ambitions! It was time she accepted that her agenda was not his. Accepted that his agenda was filled with women of a quite different category from marriageable heiresses.

His eyes went to Carrie's sleeping form. In repose, she looked lovelier than ever, the tumbled swathe of her golden hair lavish across the pillow, her slender nakedness only half covered by the sheet he had thrown back in rising, the twin mounds of her breasts delectably exposed, her long lashes sweeping her pale cheeks, her mouth bee-stung from his kisses.

Oh, yes, the image of enticing loveliness, indeed!

A complete contrast to Anastasia Savarkos. He must have

encountered her any number of times at various social engagements in Athens over the years, but her dark, austere looks and style were a world away from Carrie's fair, soft beauty. Her personality was serious—studious, even—and her eyes had a wintry glitter in them. But whilst Alexeis could appreciate Anastasia Savarkos's style of looks objectively, they did not appeal to him personally.

His eyes went to Carrie's sleeping form again, flickering over her. His mouth twisted. Did his mother really imagine that he would abandon what he had here to sit through some painful formal dinner while she went through the matchmaking preliminaries with Anastasia Savarkos? But of course his mother had no idea where he was, or who with.

Supposing she did?

The words formed in his mind before he could stop them. He stilled.

They came again.

Suppose he made it crystal-clear to his mother, for once and for all, that he had absolutely no interest in Anastasia Savarkos—or any other potential bride she wheeled out for him? Suppose he finally and irrefutably brought home to her that what he wanted were liaisons of the type he was enjoying now? Nothing else. Would that at last persuade her to abandon her unreal expectations? To put aside her pointless hopes for him? Stop her seeking out ever more heiresses to try and tempt him to marriage?

His thoughts raced ahead in his mind, and he let them do so. Let them reach the end point, the conclusion, as tempting to him as the woman that lay sleeping in his bed.

Suppose I go to Lefkali—but not alone?

His eyes flickered over Carrie's sleeping figure yet again. *Why not? Why not do it?*

It would tick every box. It would bring home to his mother

once and for all that he was not in the market for an heiress bride, and it would also mean—a smile of satisfaction played around his mouth now—that he would not have to do without what he wanted: Carrie at his side, exclusively.

Decision gripped him. Yes, it was the perfect solution. He lowered himself down on the bed, and gently ran his hand along Carrie's peach-skinned thigh. She stirred, waking drowsily. He bent and kissed her softly on the mouth as she awoke, her eyes going, as they always did, straight to him, clinging to his.

He drew back a little and smiled down at her, his hand still warm on her thigh.

'There's been a change of plan,' he said.

CHAPTER SIX

CARRIE sat in her wide leather seat on the executive jet, gazing out of the window at the landscape far, far below. Relief filled her. In her head she still heard Alexeis's voice on the yacht, sounding almost brusque. It had filled her with such dread.

'A change of plan.' Even as she'd heard the words she had felt her heart plummet. This was it. He was sending her away. Finishing it. But it hadn't been that at all. Instead, the change of plan had consisted not of sailing across the Tyrrhenian Sea to Sardinia, as Alexeis had originally told her, but flying to an island off the western coast of Greece.

'It will only be for a couple of nights,' he'd said. 'Then we'll go to Sardinia, as planned.'

He hadn't explained why there had been a change of plan, and Carrie hadn't asked. She accepted that Alexeis took travel for granted, and for him it was no big deal. She was just grateful he was taking her with him—because one day, she knew, with that feeling of a stone being lodged inside her, he would not. One day he would put her back on a plane for London, kiss her goodbye, and she would be gone. Out of his life for ever. And she would never see him again.

Claws pincered in her stomach. Urgently she tried to stop

them. She mustn't feel like that—she mustn't! Yes, she was bowled over by him, by what was happening to her—what woman would not be?—but she knew Alexeis saw her and their relationship as merely temporary, as she herself did. How could it be anything more? For all her stunned wonder at what was happening to her, she had kept her head on her shoulders. Alexeis Nicolaides was the biggest box of Belgian chocolates in the world—but that was *all* he was. All he must be. All she must let him be…

This was a fantasy—nothing more. Reality was in England, where it had always been for her. Not jetting around the world with Alexeis Nicolaides!

As ever, when her thoughts were of Alexeis and he was there, her eyes sought him out. He was sitting on the other side of the plane from her, surrounded by papers, his laptop on the table. He always worked when he travelled, and she could see the sense of it. She let him be, not seeking his attention or conversation. Now, though, he seemed more preoccupied than usual, a line of tension between his brows, his expression sombre. Her father had been similar; just a glance at him had told her when he did not want to be disturbed. She turned her head, looking out through the wide porthole, gazing down at Italy, thousands of feet below.

Across the aisle, Alexeis's eyes flickered briefly to her. He always knew instinctively when she was looking at him. Not that she ever wanted to gain his attention—she was astute enough to know when he needed to concentrate on something. That was something else he appreciated about her.

A flicker of disquiet went through him, lacing through a mood that was already not good. He didn't want to go to Lefkali. Not just because he didn't want his holiday with Carrie interrupted, but because, despite its outward beauty, Lefkali hid an inner ugliness. It had been there that his parents' marriage had broken up so dramatically, with the discovery that his father's young mistress had been pregnant. His mother had insisted that the opulent Nicolaides summer villa should be part of her divorce settlement, despite it being the scene of her husband's betrayal.

Alexeis couldn't understand why. Had she clung on to the villa just as she'd clung on to being *Kyria* Nicolaides, never remarrying so she could remind the world she was the original, the first, of her faithless husband's wives?

He pulled his mind away. He loved his mother, but pitied her deeply. He could not fall in with her aspirations and obsessions, and he needed her to stop plaguing him with them once and for all.

His eyes again rested on Carrie. Her beautiful profile was turned from him slightly, the lovely line of her graceful neck accentuating the slender beauty of her body. The thread of disquiet came again. Was it fair to her to use her in this way, to send a clear message to his mother? A glint of hardness formed in his eyes, and the memory of Carrie asking him about settling down came into his consciousness. Perhaps it would be good for Carrie, as well as his mother, to understand her place in his life…

Compunction nipped at him. No, that was unfair of him. She had shown absolutely no sign of trying to take advantage of their liaison, of seeking to make anything more of it than he was prepared to allow. She knew her place in his life— accepted it, appreciated it. As for the role she would play at his mother's dinner party—well, she would be unaware of it. It hadn't bothered her on their travels to be the woman he had chosen for his bed, so why should it be any different on Lefkali?

All the same, the thread of disquiet did not quite unknot itself. He shrugged it aside. Lefkali was an interruption, nothing more. He would attend his mother's ill-conceived dinner party, send his message home, then leave for Sardinia the next day and that would be that. Resolute once more, he returned to his work.

The flight across Italy did not take long, and their journey was completed by helicopter from the small airport in Epirus. Carrie was absorbed, craning her neck to see the hilly offshore islands, their bare peaks protruding from lush dark green woodland, the land lapped by an azure sea. Lefkali, so it seemed, was only a small island, lying offshore from a much larger one, with scattered villas at widely spaced intervals.

The helicopter veered around the southernmost point, starting its descent, and Carrie's breath caught as they passed a gleaming marbelline villa, set in a series of terraces leading down to a wide beach. But the helicopter did not land there, instead going over a low neck of land at one end of the beach to reveal a much smaller dwelling, tucked back from a tiny stony beach. It touched down on a wide driveway, leading from the villa through beautiful landscaped gardens.

As she got out, Alexeis automatically helped her down. Carrie felt the air was warmer, fragrant with the scent of maquis from the aromatic vegetation. The beach house was small, but very prettily set, with bougainvillaea clambering over its gleaming white surface, and pots of flowers everywhere. A little stone terrace looked right over the beach, and the sea could only be a stone's throw from where you might sit having breakfast under a parasol.

She was enchanted.

'It's so pretty.' She smiled as she went with Alexeis into the villa.

He didn't answer, and as she glanced at him Carrie realised

the set of his shoulders was tense, his expression closed. She said nothing more. He obviously wasn't in the mood for trivial conversation.

What he *was* in the mood for, she swiftly discovered, once their bags had been brought inside and the helicopter had left, was sex. She was in a single bedroom much larger than she'd expected one to be in such a small villa, decorated in a style she privately considered overdone, when he walked in. He looked at her a moment, as she looked round from hanging up the beautiful clothes that were now hers to wear for Alexeis.

For a moment he held her gaze, and then rapidly, briefly, his gaze went around the room, before coming back to her. His shoulders, she could see, were still set tensely.

'Are—are you all right?' she ventured.

He nodded, giving her a perfunctory smile.

'OK…' she answered, feeling unaccountably put down. Knowing she was being over-sensitive, she went on unpacking. Suddenly he was right there behind her, his hands closing over her upper arms and turning her around.

'I'm sorry,' he said. 'My mind was elsewhere.' He removed a garment from her hands and dropped it carelessly onto an open drawer in the huge wardrobe unit. 'Leave that. One of the maids will do it later.' He drew her against him, just holding her for a moment. She let her head rest against his chest, quietly.

He slid his fingers under her chin, and tilted her face upward to him.

'You never complain, do you?' he said. There was an odd note in his voice, a quizzical expression in his eye—and something more too.

Her eyes widened in genuine surprise. 'What on earth could I have to complain about? I'm living in paradise!' She smiled diffidently up at him.

The strange look came into his eye again. 'Yes, well, don't forget there are serpents in paradise. Beautiful places can hide dark feelings.' He paused. 'Bad memories,' he finished. His expression shifted again. His voice changed. 'And bad memories should be exorcised. By the most effective means possible.'

His fingers slid to play with the tender lobe of her ear, and Carrie could see the familiar, oh, so deliciously familiar glint start in his eyes.

'You really are so very lovely,' he murmured. 'How could anyone resist you?' A crooked smile pulled at his mouth, making Carrie's breath catch. 'I know I can't,' he said, and lowered his mouth to hers. 'And why should I?' he murmured again, as his lips glided smoothly, sensuously, across hers and his arm tightened around her.

He drew her down on to the bed and started to make love to her. She responded as she always did—with ardency, eagerness, and—as she did every time—with absolute wonder that this was actually happening to her.

And yet when at length she lay in the circle of his arms, her clothes long gone, and his too, her heart still beating like a wild bird, she knew there had been something different about the way Alexeis had taken her. He had been more demanding, more urgent—as if, she thought, he had needed the release.

She eased herself round in his loose embrace to look at him. Whatever release he had found, the tension was now back. His brows were drawn together, the fantastic planes of his face tautened and his eyes were closed.

Tentatively she lifted herself away from him, resting on her elbow, and then, feeling bold, curved her free hand over the mesh of sinew, bone and muscle between his neck and the cusp of his shoulder, starting to knead softly into the flesh. For a second he tensed more, and then, as she continued to work gently over the area, she saw his face begin to relax. He shifted his position, so that he was lying flat on his back, his eyes still closed, and Carrie levered herself to a half-sitting position, freeing her other hand to knead his other shoulder.

He murmured something. It was in Greek, and he repeated it in English.

'That feels good.'

She smiled and kept going. 'I'll do your back if you turn over,' she said.

He obliged, aligning himself for her, arms stretched out over his head, and Carrie started to massage him, working gently into the knots and muscles along his shoulderblades and spine.

His musculature was superb—honed and planed—and his skin tanned and smooth.

He gave a sigh of satisfaction as she worked over his back. 'You should be a masseuse,' he said, half into the pillow.

She smiled again. 'And you should be a male model,' she said lightly.

He half lifted his head and cocked an interrogative eyebrow at her, a decided glint in his eye.

'But you're far too masculine,' she assured him. 'You can just be a movie star instead.'

He gave a grunt of amusement. 'I meant it about you taking up massage,' he said. 'You're really very good at it. Have you ever thought of it?'

Carrie laughed. 'No. Never.'

'You should,' he said. 'There must be places you can train from scratch, without any qualifications.'

Carrie paused a moment and frowned, then resumed. 'Um, it's not really my thing.'

'Well, it has to beat waitressing, surely?' said Alexis. 'And, if you prefer, you could always just massage women. Though I can guarantee you'd have men queuing around the block to get a massage from you!'

There was an odd look on Carrie's face, and Alexeis suddenly felt bad. He rolled over, taking her hand in his.

'I'm sorry—I didn't mean it to sound like that! Just that you're a beautiful girl, that's all. Beautiful and very…' he paused, trying to find the right word '—very sweet,' he said. He lifted her hand to his mouth and kissed her knuckle. 'Very sweet. And,' the glint showed in his eye again, and his free hand curved around the nape of her neck, drawing her down to him '—very, very desirable. That massage quite definitely had restorative powers…'

It was quite some time before those powers were exhausted.

'Will you look,' Alexeis said, 'particularly beautiful tonight for me? Will you wear the turquoise chiffon? And the diamond necklace?'

He was smiling down at Carrie as she sat doing her make-up for the evening at the vanity unit in the vast *en suite* bathroom of the villa's bedroom. Both bathroom and bedroom seemed oversized to her, given the scale of the villa, and the bathroom especially seemed very opulent—replete with Jacuzzi, sunken bath and sauna. She wondered about the whole place. It seemed a bit too flash even for Alexeis. The hotels they had stayed at in London, New York and Milan had all been older, more traditional luxury hotels, with classic style—quite the opposite of flash.

But she'd made no comment—it was none of her business, and anyway she was glad Alexeis seemed to have lost the tension he'd had earlier on. Perhaps that massage really had helped.

Had he really meant that comment about her taking it up

professionally? Surely he'd been joking, hadn't he? Surely he knew that she could never be a masseuse? But, whatever, he'd seen her reaction, and his apology had surprised her. More than surprised her.

She felt a little lump form in her throat.

He called me sweet...

It was weird—Alexeis complimented her a lot, telling her she looked beautiful, and desirable, and yet the way he had said that had meant far more to her.

And of course if he wanted her to wear the turquoise chiffon, she would do just that. It was a beautiful gown—absolutely breathtaking. Folds and folds of filmy chiffon, in a very simple style, falling from a high waist and a tiny pleated bodice. *Very* tiny, actually, only just covering the swell of her breasts and leaving all the rest of her bare. She wore it with a shawl of the same chiffon, in a slightly deeper hue. It was almost transparent, but it acted as a veil, as well as being beautifully elegant over her shoulders, arms and elbows.

The dress was, she thought privately, a bit overkill just for dining here at the villa—especially if she added the exquisite diamond necklace that she was almost too terrified to wear, knowing how valuable it must be. But she had to admit that the dress was one of her favourites, and so she was glad to wear it for Alexeis—glad to look beautiful for him.

She finished her make-up, and left the bathroom to Alexeis. By the time he emerged, white towel wrapped around his lean waist in a way that made her breath catch, as it always did, his dark hair still damp and his jaw freshly shaved, she was already gowned and had her hair coiled into the kind of simple chignon that she could manage on her own.

His eyes glinted as he looked her over.

'Perfect,' he said, and nodded. 'Apart from—' his focus narrowed suddenly '—the hair.' Before she realised it, he'd crossed to her and drawn the pins out of her chignon, so that her hair tumbled down her back in a pale swathe.

'Keep it loose,' he said.

Then he busied himself getting swiftly dressed. He put on a tuxedo, and Carrie smiled to herself that he was taking the trouble even for dinner together. Would they eat on the little terrace overlooking the sea? She hoped so—it was warm out, and the sea was glinting with moonlight.

She felt a little thrill of anticipation. Oh, this would be something for the memory box! Dining with Alexeis under the Adriatic moon, in the warmth of the Greek night. Just the two of them…

He was fastening his dress tie, obviously nearly ready, and she picked up the filmy transparent shawl and started to drape it around her shoulders.

'You won't need that,' said Alexis, and dropped it back on the bed. 'OK, let's go.'

'Go?' She sounded surprised.

'We're invited for dinner,' said Alexeis.

She looked at him uncertainly. She had assumed they were eating here. She felt disappointment shaft through her. She didn't want to go out to dinner—she would have far preferred to stay here, in the intimacy of the villa, and be alone, just her and Alexeis.

He was steering her from the room now, and as they walked out of the villa, along a path through the gardens, Carrie found herself wishing she had the shawl around her. Not because it was cold—the night was warm and balmy— but because she felt exposed without its cover. If she'd been just going to dine with Alexeis it would not have mattered. But the dress was very low cut—very *décolleté*.

'Could—could I just go back and get my wrap, Alexeis?' she asked.

He glanced down at her. 'We're running late as it is,' he said, and kept walking. His voice seemed brusque, and Carrie found herself flinching inwardly. Then she steeled herself. She really mustn't be such a sensitive little flower.

Anyway, maybe she'd imagined the brusqueness. Because as the path lead slightly upwards, across the neck of land cutting off the tiny bay the villa was on, he suddenly stopped. He turned to her. Moonlight was streaming down on them, and the air was rich with the sound of cicadas all around. It was a beautiful Mediterranean night. He cupped her cheeks with his hands, his fingers lacing into the loose waves of her hair. She looked up at him helplessly as his gaze poured into hers.

'Lovely Carrie,' he said, his voice low, his eyes working over her. 'So very, very lovely…'

Her lips parted. He bent his head and kissed her.

It was a deep, sensual kiss, arousing in her the stirrings and longings that were so easily aroused whenever he touched her, caressed her. She was swept away, borne off on a tide of longing and wonder and deep sensuality. She clung to him, hands pressing against his chest, her mouth moving beneath his. She could feel, hot and hectic, the pulse throb at her throat, feel her breasts swelling too, their tips hardening against his chest.

When he released her she was breathless, boneless. She could only gaze at him, eyes wide, lips parted, filled with desire for him—unstoppable, irresistible desire.

Oh, what is it that he does to me? How can I feel like this?

The questions flared in her mind, but she could not think, could not do anything but be awash with the feelings he aroused in her. More than feelings.

He gave a smile. It was one of satisfaction.

Then he cupped his hand under her elbow and led her

around the path as it opened up on the far side of the neck of land.

Carrie caught her breath—but from a quite different cause.

It was the villa she'd seen from the helicopter, built dramatically into the slope of the land so that the lower terraces seemed to be almost cascading down to the sea, splashed with golden brightness from hidden lights.

They were level with one of the terraces, and Carrie realised that the path they were on led straight to it. Alexeis steered her forward, and on to the smooth, stone tiles.

'This way,' he said, and walked around the corner of the villa. The terrace opened up, and she saw the azure glow of an underlit swimming pool. Then they were walking past it and up some marble steps to an upper terrace. As they emerged she took in an impression of people, a buzz of conversation, soft music, lights, and through huge French windows a lavishly set dinner table in a room behind the terrace. Alexeis led her forward. His hand on her elbow tightened.

Carrie saw a woman start forward from the others there. Start forward—and stop dead.

Suddenly everyone there had stopped, stilled. She heard Alexeis speak. His tones were smooth. He spoke Greek, and she did not understand a word he said.

But the woman who had started forward and then stopped seemed to have frozen. She was clearly in middle age, very slim, with features that were strong rather than beautiful, but she was formidably elegant in a long dark dress, her hair beautifully coiffed and tinted.

A little way behind her was another female, a generation younger. She was wearing a high-necked sleeveless dress, in olive-green silk. She was dark-haired, with her hair in a tight chignon. She had a rope of pearls around her neck, and pearl drops in her ears. She had striking features which drew Carrie's eye.

But she, too, was standing as still as a statue.

Alexeis walked forward. He seemed unconcerned by the fact that everyone had stopped. He walked up to the formidably elegant middle-aged woman, who was, Carrie gathered, the owner of the lavish villa they were visiting. She was also, she realised with a mind that could pay the fact no attention, vaguely familiar, though she would have remembered seeing her before, she knew. Alexeis said something in Greek and bent to kiss her immobile cheek. Then he straightened.

He smiled. Half at the woman, half at Carrie.

'This is Carrie,' he said in English. 'She's staying with me at the beach house. I know you won't mind me bringing her.'

For a moment longer the tableau held, then Alexeis spoke again, moving forward, bringing Carrie with him. He came up to the young woman in the olive-green dress and said something to her in Greek. Her face, Carrie could see, had become as immobile as the older woman's. She made no response to whatever it was that Alexeis had said, and then, as if it was an effort, inclined her head and made some single-worded reply. Her immobility and scant reply did not seem to bother him.

Instead, he beckoned a manservant with a tray of glasses, and took one of champagne for himself, gave another to Carrie. She took it with nerveless fingers. What on earth was going on? There were fewer people here than she'd thought, but they were the same kind of people she'd met in New York, all in evening dress and all rich-looking. The kind of people who moved in the same circles as Alexeis. But none of them had made her feel the way these people were making her feel. She bit her lip, feeling horribly self-conscious suddenly. Several of the men present were staring openly at her, and she wished desperately she had the wrap to cover herself with. Unconsciously, she pressed against Alexeis. He squeezed her elbow reassuringly, and threw a warm, smiling glance at her.

'I'm afraid we've been keeping everyone waiting for dinner,' he said.

Was that why there was an atmosphere you could cut like a knife? Because they were late? But it didn't really account for why everyone was staring at her the way they were. Hanging on to Alexeis's sleeve, still feeling hideously self-conscious and awkward, she let him take her through towards the dining table, to take her seat beside him.

She got through the meal, which was long and elaborate, the best she could. Which was badly. But whilst she might want, overpoweringly, to leap to her feet and run back to the beach villa as fast as her evening gown and sandals would let her, she knew she couldn't. Just couldn't.

Why was everyone covertly—and not so covertly—still staring at her? What had she done that was so terrible? Was it the dress? Was it too low cut compared with any other woman's there? But if so why on earth had Alexeis not told her to wear something else, or at least to keep her wrap on? She was the only woman with her hair down, too, and that made her even more self-conscious. She kept flicking it back over her shoulders, trying to keep it out of the way, wishing she could just pin it up and be done with it. But whenever she touched it, it seemed to draw eyes—male and female. Some of their glares went to her throat, where the glitter of the diamonds that Alexeis had wanted her to wear for the evening was cold on her skin. What was wrong with diamonds with this dress? OK, so some of the women were wearing pearls, but at least one had a very prominent ruby necklace, and another had a large sapphire and diamond brooch on her opulent bosom.

Or was it, she realised, with a gradually chilling hollow feeling, *her* they were objecting to? Was that it? Not just because they were late, but because Alexeis hadn't told his hostess he was bringing her with him? Was that the offence? But, if so, it was hardly her fault—she hadn't invited herself. Nor was it her fault that she didn't speak Greek—she didn't speak Italian, either, but no one in Milan had frozen her out like this, even if they hadn't exactly chattered away to her either.

No, something was wrong. But she didn't know what, and all she could do, she knew, was to ignore it the best she could, get on with the meal—hardly tasting the food because all appetite had left her, drinking as little as possible. The conversation, such as it was, was entirely in Greek, and no one spoke to her, including Alexeis. Between courses she sat tense and miserable, wondering why Alexeis had bothered to bring her at all. He could easily have left her at the villa and not brought her along to his opulent neighbour's party. Anyway, she was an extra female here—she could see everyone else had a partner. Apart, she realised, from the tall girl in the olive-green dress, who was sitting at the far end of the table from Alexeis, next to her hostess.

How Carrie managed to stick it out to the bitter end, she didn't know. But eventually, after what seemed an eternity of misery, there was a general rising from the table. Alexeis was taking her arm again, and leading her forward, towards their hostess. He said something to her in Greek, to which the woman gave a tight-lipped reply. Then he grazed her cheek with his lips and drew Carrie away. She didn't say anything, focussing only on not tripping in her high-heeled sandals as they made their way along the path back to the little beach villa.

As they entered Alexeis turned to her. His expression remote. 'Excuse me, but I have to check my e-mails,' he said.

He strode off, leaving her to walk slowly to the bedroom, where she started to get undressed. She felt horrible. Wrong.

For the first time since she had encountered Alexeis, been swept away with him, the fantasy suddenly seemed to have gone flat.

Alexeis stared at the screen on his laptop, seeing nothing that was there. Well, his method had been effective, that was for certain. Brutal, but effective. He had signalled, loud and clear, that he was not in the marriage market. Carrie's presence at his side had seen to that!

But it had not been a pleasant experience. Anastasia, not unnaturally, had taken umbrage—but that was too bad. It would at least persuade her he was not a suitable husband for her. His mother, of course, had been rigid with anger, chagrin and disapproval. And that was too bad too. It had been unfortunate that Carrie had inevitably drawn the kind of attention from the male guests that she had, but then he and Carrie would be leaving in the morning, so she would not encounter them again.

He glanced distastefully around him at the opulent décor in the over-decorated gold and white lounge. The sooner he was out of here the better. An angry exhalation escaped him.

He had the life he wanted—and that would do very well for him, thank you. Now he most fervently hoped his mother would finally accept that, and stop plaguing him.

He closed down his laptop. This time tomorrow he would be in Sardinia, Carrie at his side. There were no more impediments in the way. He would resume the life he wanted—no complications, no pressures, no expectations.

Just Carrie, to make him feel good.

He got to his feet, mood already improved, and headed for bed. She was asleep already, he could see, tucked up in an almost foetal position, clearly out for the count. Just for once he decided not to wake her. Right now he didn't feel like sex. He just felt like holding her.

To make him feel good.

CHAPTER SEVEN

CARRIE turned over on to her stomach, letting the warmth of the sunshine seep into her as she lay on a padded sunbed in front of the beach house. She was on her own, and for once she was glad. She'd slept heavily, having taken some painkillers for the tension headache that had started to grind around her temples after the gruelling ordeal of that awful dinner party. The pills had knocked her out, and she'd been unaware that Alexeis had come to bed. Then, as the bright morning sunlight had pressed through the unsuitably ornate drapes of the bedroom, he had hunkered down beside the bed, roused her by softly shaking her shoulder, and said, 'I have to go up to the villa, but I won't be too long. We'll leave for Sardinia as soon as I'm back.'

There had been a constraint in his voice she had picked up on even through her drowsiness, but she had not questioned him. Then he'd gone. Now her thoughts were troubled, but she didn't want to think. She also felt queasy as well. Perhaps that ordeal of a meal had affected her digestion, as well as her spirits? She shifted restlessly, wishing she didn't feel this way, when she was so incredibly lucky to be lying on a Mediterranean beach, living in luxury, instead of slaving away in London doing boring, poorly paid work she didn't want to do.

And so incredibly lucky to have Alexeis—

She waited for the familiar warm glow that always came when she thought of him, conjured his image in her mind. But it did not come. Instead, she saw again in her mind the sombre outline of his profile as he'd sat on the plane from Italy, and the abstracted remoteness he had displayed as they'd walked back from that ghastly dinner party last night.

She felt unease seep through her.

The splash of water and the crunch of pebbles made her start. She half lifted herself on her elbow, the hair scooped around her neck tumbling over her shoulder, her bikini top dipping low over the swell of her breasts, and looked up. There was a shadow against the sun. Tall and masculine. It stepped forward towards her.

'Well, well—so here she is. Alexeis's delectable blonde bimbo, in all her bare, sexy, sunkissed flesh...'

The voice was a drawl, the language English, and the accent that of a fellow native.

Carrie stared. She couldn't do anything else. The figure moved forward and dropped into a casual crouch right beside her sunbed. She blinked. He was young, tanned, with dark hair and a pair of piercing blue eyes that looked straight at her.

Eyes that were stripping her of her bikini.

Before she realised what was happening, he'd reached out a hand and smoothed it, brazenly, over her rounded bottom.

'Oh, nice—very nice indeed,' the drawl came again. The piercing blue eyes came back to her face, 'I don't suppose that, considering you put out for Alexeis, you'd care to put out for me as well, would you?'

He cocked an interrogative eyebrow at her, his hand still resting on her bottom.

Carrie slapped him.

It was instinct, and it was raw outrage. The man reeled back exaggeratedly, and got to his feet.

He thrust his hands into the pockets of his shorts and looked down at her as she scrambled to her feet, on the far side of the sunbed, backing away and grabbing her sarong to her front.

'I can run to diamonds, too,' the man said, in that same drawl, his eyes never leaving her. 'I might not have quite the credit balance that Alexeis has, but I can definitely run to diamonds.' His eyes stripped her again. 'And you'd be worth it, angel—oh, definitely worth it.' His voice husked.

He started to walk towards her. There was purpose in his gait.

Panic knifed through Carrie. She dropped down, snatching up the biggest stone to hand, and, straightening, hefted it back.

'Keep away!' she cried. Her voice was high-pitched with fear. 'Keep away from me!' She threw the stone at him. It missed completely, and she ducked down to snatch up another one.

The man stopped. His expression changed.

'Are you mad?' he demanded.

The air was like glass in Carrie's lungs, her heart pounding with panic. 'Keep away from me!' she cried again.

The man suddenly laughed shortly. 'Oh, for God's sake, cool it. I won't lay a finger on you. I just wanted to see you for myself after all the trouble you've caused. Look, put the bloody stone down, will you? The next time you might aim to miss me and kill me!'

She didn't move—fear still paralysed her. The man's expression changed again. Lost a fraction of its hard edge as he held his hands out in a submissive gesture.

'Look, sugar, cool it—OK? You're quite safe, I promise you. I don't jump women.' He gave a throwaway laugh. 'Hell, they usually jump *me*! And, like I said, I just wanted to see you for myself. You can't blame me for that—the old witch is just about sticking pins into your effigy for what you did last night!'

Slowly, Carrie lowered the stone.

'Who are you?' she asked.

The panic was subsiding now, and she was actually able to look at the man, take in his features. They seemed familiar. She frowned slightly. Where had he come from? The villa? But she hadn't seem him last night. The man raised his eyebrows. Again, it was a curiously familiar gesture, yet she'd never seen him before in her life.

'So, Alexeis hasn't bothered to fill you in, I see? Well, why should he? You're only a bit-player, after all. And your main theatre of action is his bed, obviously. Which, like I say, when he's done with you, you can swap for mine any time, no problem.'

The piercing blue eyes removed her clothes again. Carrie's hand tightened automatically on the stone, which she had not relinquished. Her panic might have gone, but another emotion was taking its place.

'Don't speak to me like that!' Anger flashed across her face.

The man was completely unfazed by it, merely cocking an eyebrow again.

'Were you hoping for more? Sorry to disappoint you. Like me, my big brother Alexeis doesn't go in for long-term relationships.' The drawl sharpened suddenly. 'Nor does he go in for bimbos, either.' The blue eyes narrowed. 'You are definitely, very definitely, not his type—so he must have been planning that stunt of his all along. When did he pick you up, anyway?'

Carrie only heard one phrase.

'Big brother? Alexeis? He's your *brother*?' she said slowly.

She stared at the man. He was younger than Alexeis, but not much, maybe two or three years. That was why he seemed so familiar, despite the blue eyes.

And the obnoxious personality.

'The very same. The autocratic, arrogant, almighty number one Nicolaides son. With a witch for a mother.'

'Witch?'

He gave that short laugh again, with no humour in it.

'You didn't think so? After meeting her last night? Not that she'd have actually acknowledged your existence. She's very good at blanking people—especially people she doesn't want to exist.' Something moved in his eyes. It was anger—brief, sudden, and gone.

Carrie was staring at him. What was he saying? What could he *possibly* be saying?

'I don't understand,' she said.

He smiled. It wasn't a very nice one. 'Yes, well, as the resident bimbo you're not supposed to. You're just supposed to lie back and let the lordly Alexeis Nicolaides get his regular nightly oats—in exchange for some pretty dresses and some even prettier shiny trinkets, of course. I'm sure you don't come cheap, babe.'

She gripped the stone tighter than ever, and felt her arm begin to jerk upwards. Then, out of nowhere, the blue eyes changed completely. The ice in them went. So did the unpleasant smile.

'*Christos,* why am I laying into you?' He gave a heavy, angry sigh, spreading his hands wide. 'Hell, last night played right into my hands.' He stopped, but Carrie had had enough.

'I haven't the faintest idea what you are on about,' she said shortly. 'If you really are Alexeis's brother, then I suggest you go and find him. He's up at the villa, but I'm sure he'll be back soon.'

The laugh came again. Still without humour.

'Not if the witch has anything to do with it. She'll be bending his ear right now. Laying into him. He might be her darling son, but he sure as hell blotted his copybook big time last night, trotting you out like that—'

Yet again, there was only one part of what this brother of Alexeis was saying.

'What did you say?' she said in a hollow voice.

He looked blank a moment.

'Didn't you think she would? Lay into him? After what he did to her last night? She'd built up really big hopes this time around—if any woman would be a feather in her cap for her precious son it would be the brand-new Savarkos heiress.' His mouth twisted cynically. 'You can't blame her for trying—for wanting Alexeis to snap up such a prize. The Savarkos money would really impress the hell out of our esteemed father.'

Carrie was staring, trying to make sense—sense out of something she couldn't believe she was hearing. 'Are you saying—' her voice was hollow '—that…the woman in the villa, at the dinner party last night, is Alexeis's mother?'

The blue eyes stared right at her.

'He didn't tell you who she was?'

Slowly, Carrie shook her head. A huge lump was forming in her throat, harder than the stone gripped in her nerveless hand.

Alexeis's brother said something in Greek. It didn't sound polite. He came towards her, and this time Carrie didn't back away defensively, didn't get ready to heft her stone at him. She was blinking, the stone in her throat.

Could it be *true*? Alexeis had taken her to dinner at his mother's house and he hadn't told her?

But *why*?

'You haven't a clue, have you?' The voice and the expression had changed again, were half pitying, half contemptuous. 'Look, come and sit down. It's a tad complicated, so you'll need to put your single brain cell in.'

She felt her arm being taken as she was steered back to the sunlounger, and lowered down on it. Then he was sitting down beside her. Automatically she edged away, looking at him with baleful wariness. He gave his cynical, humourless smile.

'OK—listen up. Even bimbos should get a chance to know when they're being set up. So—here goes.' He took a heavy breath, and started. 'I'm Yannis, Alexeis's kid brother. Alexeis is only my half-brother. His mother is Berenice Nicolaides— aka the witch. When Alexeis was a toddler, old man Nicolaides got his mistress pregnant. Since Berenice couldn't have any more children, my not very esteemed father decided to dump his wife and marry his floozy. It caused a hell of a scandal, apparently, and sent Berenice nuclear. Even more so when the old man moved said floozy into the love-nest he'd just had built for her.'

Yannis nodded at the beach house. 'Been wondering why it looks like a tart's boudoir on the inside? Because it *is* one, that's why.' His mouth tightened a moment, and that angry look shot into his eyes, then it was gone again, and the cynical look was back in them.

'Anyway, the divorce came through just before yours truly.' He gave an exaggerated and mocking bow. 'Not a bastard after all. Something the witch has never forgiven me for. Instead, not only was I the official number two son, but, worst of all, the floozy became the number two Kyria Nicolaides.'

Carrie swallowed. She edged away again. There was distaste in her eyes.

'You speak of your own mother as a…a…'

Yannis's mouth twisted. The flash came into the blue eyes again.

'I'm quoting the witch. And my esteemed father, of course. Oh, my mother was *Kyria* Nicolaides in name, but that was all. To him, she was still just a mistress.' He took another rough intake of breath. 'So, that's the set-up. The witch hates my guts—and it's pretty mutual by now—and she hates the old man's guts as well, thirty years on. Her number one goal in life is to see me cut out of any of the Nicolaides fortune to ensure Alexeis gets the lot. She thinks that hooking him an heiress will give him more clout—plus, of course—' the cynical look was back in his face '—the prospect of a grandson. So she regularly trots out likely candidates for him, to see if she can finally get him nailed. To his credit, Alexeis doesn't bite—in fact, he's getting increasingly irritated by it.' The blue eyes latched back onto her. 'Which is where you come in. Obviously Alexeis decided it was time his dear mama finally got the message, loud and clear—and you were it, sugar. Why marry when he's got a hot little number like you warming him up at night?'

He got to his feet. Carrie went on sitting there; she felt she couldn't move. Yannis glanced down at her. There was still that expression of cynicism and rough sympathy on his face, but now tinged with faint impatient contempt.

'Look, don't take it so bad. OK, he used you—but girls like you know the score. Hell, I should know! Get what you can, while you can. Alexeis only picked you because he knew you'd be ideal for last night's little soap opera. Now I'm afraid you'll probably be surplus to requirements.'

Carrie lifted her head.

'Would you mind going back to wherever you came from?' Her voice was stiff, and she could hardly get the words out. The stone in her throat seemed to be getting larger all the time. So was the emotion building in her head.

Yannis shrugged, as if her reaction had riled him. 'So Alexeis had an agenda? Big deal. No point being narked about it. It's not like it's hearts and flowers between you, so—'

'Will you please just *go*?'

Finally, he went. She watched, face stiff as a board, while he sauntered crunchingly down over the stones to step into a dinghy moored on the beach. She watched him slowly move off, her hands gripping each other tightly in her lap.

He was almost level with the headland when she heard footsteps behind her. She turned, jerking round to see Alexeis striding down the path from the villa—not looking at her, but at the dinghy out to sea. She saw a look of surprise turn swiftly to angry exasperation. Then his eyes were going to her.

'I'm sorry I had to abandon you,' he said. 'Are you all packed, or shall I send for a maid from the villa?'

His voice was tight, abstracted. But she was hardly in a state to notice. She forced herself to answer, conscious that she was gripping her sarong around her with all her strength.

'No. It will only take me five minutes,' she managed to get out. Her voice was jerky. She couldn't look at him. The stone inside her was too big. Her eyes flickered past him as she headed indoors. She could hear Alexeis coming in behind her. Everything seemed to be coming and going. The walls of the house were moving slowly in and out. She stood a moment, hand on the doorjamb, trying to steady herself.

'Carrie—are you all right?' Alexeis's voice was sharp.

She blinked, hanging onto the door, trying to make herself focus, then suddenly, out of nowhere, an abdominal cramp doubled her up. She gasped.

'Carrie!'

Her free arm was being taken, her weight supported, but the cramp came again, making her cry out.

'Bathroom—' she managed to get out.

He helped her there, and she staggered in, half doubled up, cramping pain shooting through her. She shut the door on him, not wanting him to see, then collapsed down on the toilet seat. The cramp came again, and she had to bite her lip to stop crying out. Then, blessedly, it passed. She waited, feeling sweat beading on her forehead.

'Carrie?'

'I'm—I'm OK,' she breathed. She stood up; it had been cramp, nothing more. But as she stood she felt dizzy again, and she dropped her head to steady herself.

And saw blood trickling down the inside of her leg.

Fog, thick and glutinous, rolled in from the periphery. Slowly and soundlessly, she folded down to the floor.

She was in bed, in a huge white room, with paintings on the walls and Venetian blinds shading the light. She was lying back on pillows, and she felt as weak as a kitten. Her feet seemed to be raised on several pillows at the foot of the bed. There was a doctor, and a nurse who was neatening the bedding. There was no one else there. The doctor nodded at the nurse and she left the room. Then he came forward, his expression neutral.

He looked at her a moment, then spoke, his English strongly accented.

'The bleeding has stopped. However, it may resume. What I have to ask you, however—' the expression of absolute neutrality deepened on his face '—is whether you deliberately induced it.'

She stared at him, understanding nothing.

'These things are possible,' the doctor said. 'And sometimes—' his voice changed slightly '—understandable. However, if that was indeed the case, then I must tell you that you will need to seek alternative medical provision.' His voice changed again. 'If the bleeding was not deliberately induced, then of course I will do everything that is possible to assist you.' His eyes were grave suddenly, and shot with sympathy. 'Although you must understand that in many cases nature will find a way, despite all our efforts, and I am sorry to tell you that you must accept that this may be the outcome.'

Carrie stared at him. What was he saying? She didn't understand.

She licked dry lips, the air as tight as steel bands in her lungs. Fear was like a knife in her brain.

'What's—what's wrong with me?'

The doctor stilled. His expression changed again.

'You did not know? Well, that is possible too. It is very early, after all.' He looked down at her, and now his expression was not neutral, but sympathetic and sad.

'You are pregnant,' he told her. 'And in very grave danger of miscarrying.'

CHAPTER EIGHT

ALEXEIS paused outside the bedroom door. He didn't want to do this. But he had no choice. He'd scooped Carrie's inert body up and carried her, as swiftly as he could, to a bed in a guest bedroom in his mother's villa. Then he'd summoned a doctor, and after he had examined Carrie had asked him outright what was wrong.

And the doctor had told him.

The shock had detonated in his brain, and his next question had been one that any man in his situation might ask. 'How many weeks?'

'It is very recent indeed. Had you not summoned me she might merely have thought it a delayed period. Many women miscarry and do not even realise they were pregnant. But in this instance—' he had looked Alexeis right in the eyes '—the miscarriage may yet have been averted—I say only *may*. Continued bed-rest is essential, and no stress whatsoever. I believe that is what may have induced her collapse.'

Alexeis's face had tightened, but he'd said nothing, only asked what medical care would be necessary. Now the doctor was gone, and he was going to have to go in and see Carrie.

He could do no less, after all.

But his thoughts, all the same, were dark. How could they not be?

Christos—what a mess! What an unholy mess!

But declaiming against it would cure nothing. He had to go in and deal with it. Deal with it the only way possible. Grimly, he pushed the door open and went inside. The blinds were still slanted, shading the room. Carrie looked very small in the double bed in the huge room, its palatial dimensions dwarfing her. She looked very out of place. As out of place as she'd looked the night before at the dinner table—Alexeis blocked the image, the memory. But it was etched in his vision all the same.

He walked slowly towards her. She was looking at him, he could see, but there was something different in her eyes.

He felt his stomach knot at the reason. What he wanted to do, above all, was walk right out of there. And keep walking.

But he couldn't. He had to face this. No choice. No choice at all.

'How are you feeling?' he asked.

Carrie looked at him. He looked the same. The same as he always did, always had. For a moment, the fraction of a second, she felt herself respond the way she always did—always had. Then, crushing her like some monstrous weight, knowledge of the truth pressed mercilessly down on her.

She wanted to shut her eyes, deny the nightmare.

Please, please don't let it be true! Please!

But it was true, for all her desperate pleas. She was pregnant. Pregnant by Alexeis. A man to whom she was nothing more than garbage—

Into her head sliced the cruel, vicious words that had been spoken to her by Alexeis's half-brother. Words that had eviscerated her.

Words that were cruelly, viciously true.

Are they? Are they true? Or are they just the unfounded accusation of someone who is clearly jealous of everything Alexeis has? Doubt flickered within her. Frail and fragile, but there all the same. She gazed into Alexeis's face. Felt that flip deep inside again.

Yes, he picked me up off the street—but I don't have to feel cheap about that! I don't, I don't! And just because the whole thing was like something out of a movie, it doesn't mean it was tacky, or tawdry. And he never treated me as if it was. And last night…last night…

Searing across the doubt came memory. Hot, humiliating memory of the night before and the hideous dinner party that Alexeis had deliberately, knowingly, purposely subjected her to. The way everyone had stared at her—including, she now knew, Alexeis's mother. All cutting her dead, as if she was something contaminated. And now she was carrying the child of the man who had held her up for the general contempt of his mother and all her guests…

She turned her head away. She could not bear to look at him. The stone in her throat was choking her. Horror swept over her. More than horror.

Yannis called me a bimbo, and he was right. That's what I am. Some stupid little airhead greedy for the high life, just wanting to live out some idiotic fantasy so I don't have to think about what I'm doing or how I'm behaving. I called it romantic when it was only sordid—sordid, cheap and tacky. And all along—

Again into her head marched all the vile, ugly things that Yannis had said to her that morning. All the harsh, horrible memories of the night before.

No wonder everyone was staring at me. They saw Alexeis Nicolaides's blonde bimbo, in a dress almost falling off her, with a tart's reward around her neck.

Into the pitiless self-condemnation emotion stabbed.

Oh, God, what a fool I've been—what a stupid, stupid little fool!

And the most hurtful thing of all was that Alexeis had thought exactly that all along. She had woven stupid, pathetic illusions over what she had done—casting an inane, rosy glow over it all—but Alexeis had never thought that. For him she had always, always been what she now so bitterly knew was the truth of it. How could it possibly be otherwise? And now the bimbo tart had done the worst thing she could ever do—she had gone and got pregnant.

Pregnant—the word tolled in her head again.

I can't be pregnant—I just can't! I can't!

But of course she could. In New York they had discussed contraception, and Carrie had told him that she wasn't on the pill. Alexeis had assured her that naturally he would take care of things, and he had always seemed to be so careful. But barrier methods of contraception were not foolproof—and now she had proof of that herself.

'Carrie?' Alexeis's voice was low. Tense. Well, it would be, wouldn't it? she thought with savage bitterness. What a total disaster for him! 'I don't want you to worry about anything,' he said. 'You must know that I will take care of you. In every way necessary.'

She went on staring at the wall, saying nothing, the stone in her throat still choking her.

'Carrie—'

The constraint in Alexeis's voice was written in giant letters. God, she thought, he must be feeling life's a bitch, to do this to him.

She heard him go on—forcing himself, she knew.

'I want you to know—' he said. 'I want you to know that if you stay pregnant, I will marry you.'

She heard the words. Heard them fall into the silence. Like stones.

She shut her eyes.

'Carrie—'

Dear God, why would he not stop? Why would he not go? Go, just go.

Alexeis gazed down at her. She had turned her head away from him, staring at the wall. Frustration bit at him.

What else did she want him to say? What else could he say? Nothing! He could say nothing! Except wish to God this had never, never happened—

But it had—and all that could be done was deal with it. Cope with it.

A hard, heavy sigh escaped from him, and he turned on his heel. He had to get out of here.

He took refuge in the office that the villa, like all the Nicolaides properties, was equipped with. He might as well get some work done. Something, anything, to pass the time. The hours that would decide his fate. A fate that hung like the sword of Damocles over his head.

A sword that would strike him, whichever way it fell.

Emotion twisted in him.

I don't want her pregnant. I want it not to be true.

Just not to be true.

God, how could it be—how *could* it be—that something so fleeting as sexual pleasure could result in this? A woman, pregnant with his child...

He veered away from the computer, yanked open the French windows that gave out on to the terrace at that level and strode out into the fresh air. Outside, everything looked so normal.

His eyes went out over the azure sea, far beyond the terrace. There was a white sail on it, heading into the wind to make a tack. It was Yannis, he knew. He had seen him that morning, when he'd come back from the painful, necessary exchange with his mother in the aftermath of the evening before. He'd cut short her tirade at him for his conduct, telling her that she only had herself to blame. He pulled his mind back. His mother's matchmaking schemes were quite unnecessary now... The biting irony of it savaged him.

His eyes lingered on the dinghy sail. Yannis took a perverse satisfaction in staying in the converted boat house by the quay on the far side of the villa. The beach house that his father had kept for equally malign purposes. Yannis's mother had been installed there. Close by, convenient, within easy walking distance of the main villa. Ramming home the heartless message to his unwanted wife that her husband preferred his pretty young mistress to her.

The mistress he'd got accidentally, unintentionally pregnant.

And in so doing, he had changed all their lives for ever.

He watched as Yannis expertly executed a close-haul fast tack and continued heading out to sea. Over thirty years had passed since Yannis's conception had changed all those lives.

Will I be standing here one day, an old man, watching my son sailing in the bay—a son whose conception was nothing more than an unintended accident?

Time seemed to gather around him—long years, past and future, coalescing into his consciousness. Life—lives—stretching out either side of him, back into the past, forward into the future, meeting at this point, this nexus of fate. The enormity of what had happened to him resonated with the past that was still here, alive and real. Because Yannis was alive and real. And so too was the future of the child in Carrie's womb. One day his adulthood would be the present, and this time of his conception the distant past—as distant as Yannis's conception that had once changed lives for ever.

A line came to him that he had read somewhere, read and dismissed. Disbelieved.

You never really understand time until you become a parent. Children create time by their very existence—they create the past and the future.

Now he knew what that meant. The child in Carrie's womb was creating his future—the future he had to face. The future that one day he would watch as an old man, looking back to this moment.

I don't want that future. I want the past. I want the past back again. The uncomplicated, enjoyable, pleasurable, familiar past. The past that existed less than a day ago…

But the past was over, and it would never come back. His life had changed for ever.

Unless—

No. He thrust the thought away. He could not think it. Could not wish it.

To do so would be monstrous…

Raggedly, he turned away, went back indoors. Back to his computer, his work, seeking oblivion.

'Alexeis!'

The voice from the doorway was imperious, demanding.

'Alexeis—I must speak to you.'

The voice came again, and he made himself respond. He could not do otherwise. He might wish to God his mother was not here, that she had left first thing that morning with all her houseguests, but she was here, and that was all there was to it. Now, as he heard his mother's voice at the door again, the words he'd thrown at her earlier, that he would never marry, bit savagely in his head, mocking him mercilessly. It seemed he was facing marriage after all…

He turned to face his mother standing, rigid, at the entrance to the office. Her face was stark.

'Is it true?' she demanded. 'The girl you brought here is pregnant?'

Alexeis could see the way her fingers were pressed against the doorjamb, white at the tips.

'Yes,' he said.

'Did you know?' Berenice Nicolaides demanded, in the same tone of voice.

Alexeis's face closed. 'No. Not until she collapsed this morning.'

'Is she miscarrying?'

'They don't know. She might be. It's threatening.'

He tensed, waiting for his mother to speak again. To say what he knew she must want to say.

Instead she came into the room, closing the door.

'What are you going to do?' she said. The demanding note had gone. Now there was only absolute neutrality. All the more punishing.

He looked at her. 'What I have to,' he answered. 'Marry her.'

She nodded slowly. Then she took a deep inhalation of breath.

'Are you certain the child is yours?'

Alexeis's mouth tightened. 'Yes,' he said tersely.

His mother's eyebrows rose sceptically.

'The pregnancy is very recent, and Carrie has been with me…for some time,' said Alexeis.

His mother's eyes shifted to the French windows—far out on the water the sail of Yannis's dinghy was still just visible. She gazed blindly a moment, then turned back to her son.

'So,' she said heavily, 'it has happened again. The same fate that destroyed me is now destroying you. God in heaven—the cruelty of it is unbearable!' Her eyes shut, then flashed open again. 'All your life I have guarded your interests, fought for you and protected you—and for what? Nothing—nothing at all!' Her face contorted. 'My own son, caught in a net cast by a gold-digging little trollop!'

'She isn't a gold-digger!' Alexeis rejected harshly. 'You know nothing about her!'

His mother's eyes flashed scornfully. 'Nothing about her? I know everything I need to know about her! I've seen her with my own eyes! You made *very* sure of that when you flaunted her here last night! *Very* clear when you "explained" to me this morning why you refuse to marry! It's glaringly obvious what kind of girl she is, and now she's got herself pregnant!' Her face contorted again.

Alexeis's hand slapped on the desktop. 'Enough! You will not speak of her in that way.' He got to his feet. His mouth pressed in a tight, white line in his stark face. He took a harsh, heavy breath, looking directly at the distraught face of his mother.

'It would be best,' he said, 'if you left. There is nothing to do here but wait.'

His mother's eyes searched his face. Then, 'And you are prepared to marry her?'

He nodded. 'I have no choice.'

Her eyes rested on him, dark and unreadable. 'No,' she said, 'you have no choice. You are an honourable man, and you will do what is right. I would expect no less of you.' Her expression changed. 'You are all I have, Alexeis. He wanted to take you from me, your father, to punish me for daring to object to being discarded like an unwanted rag. But I fought him off.' She came up to him, touched his cheek with her fingers. 'I have been blessed—blessed to have you as my son. And I will *always* guard your interests.' She gave a rare, wry smile, and Alexeis, with a tightening of his throat, thought how it changed her stark features. 'Even when you do not want me to,' she said.

She took a breath, letting her hand drop again. When she spoke again, her voice had changed. 'You defend the girl—believe she did not seek to entrap you. Why?'

'Because she is not like that.'

'You are so sure?'

'Yes.'

Her eyes narrowed. 'A woman can be cunning to disguise her true nature.'

Alexeis's brow darkened. 'She is not that kind of female. She is simply—' He broke off.

His mother's eyebrows rose, but he did not continue. His expression was taut.

'So what do you know about her—considering you may have to marry her?' his mother continued.

Alexeis shifted his weight uncomfortably. He did not want this conversation. It was a clash of worlds he had kept rigorously separate. But now those worlds had collided—catastrophically. 'I met her in London,' he said, conscious of being evasive. 'I—I don't know a great deal about her. She had recently arrived in the city from the provinces—she has no family—she works as a waitress.'

'A waitress?' Berenice Nicolaides's voice was expressionless.

'She cannot help being poor, any more than she can help being—'

He broke off.

'Entirely unsuitable to be Kyria Nicolaides?' supplied his mother. Her voice was as dry as sand.

Alexeis's jaw tightened. He was conscious of his mother's eyes resting on him. He could not read them, did not want to meet them. Thirty years of tormented family history lay in those simple words. Yannis's wretched mother had been 'unsuitable' as well...

An image burned on his retinas. Carrie last night, sitting beside him at his mother's dinner table, painting for him exactly the picture he had wanted her to. Showing his mother and all her guests exactly what he had wanted her to show them. And now he was faced with having her beside him as his wife—

Christos, had he *tried* to make it worse, to make her *more* 'unsuitable', he could not have succeeded better!

'It's—unfortunate,' he said. It was all he could say. 'She will find it…difficult…but—' and now he did look at his mother, did meet her implacable eyes '—she will have my support, my care.'

The silence rang between them. He could think of nothing more to say. Was this what his father had felt all those years ago, when his mistress had told him she was pregnant? As if something had happened to turn the world inside out and alter normality for ever, with a fall-out that would change the lives not just of his father and his mistress, but of his wife, his son—and of the child born into such disjunction, doomed to bring discord by his very existence.

And now that was happening to him.

His mother took a heavy breath again. 'If it must be, then I will stand with you. Do what I can to…' she shrugged help-lessly '…minimise the difficulties. But—'

She stopped again, then changed what she might have been going to say. She held up her hands. Her voice when she spoke again was brisk, unemotional. 'I will leave for Switzerland this evening. I am booked at the Kursaal next week, but I'll arrive early—it is no matter.' She paused a moment. 'You will—let me know, won't you?'

She did not have to say about what, nor did he ask.

'Of course.' His voice was studiously neutral. But the ex-pression in his eyes was still heavy and strained.

She nodded, saying nothing more. Then, as if on impulse, she stepped forward, gripping his arms and bestowing a swift, silent kiss on his cheek.

Then, at the door, she turned to look at him one last time. The stark look was back in her face.

'You are all I care about. Everything I do is for you—remember that.'

She did not wait for a response, only opened the door and was gone.

Heavily, Alexeis went back to his work. As he took his place at the desk, staring into the figures on the screen, he felt suddenly very alone.

He wanted someone to hold. Someone who would just let him fold his arms around her and let him draw her soft body to him, to hear her quiet breathing, inhale the scent of her clean hair, feel the slow beat of her heart.

The irony of it seemed particularly mordant.

The bedroom door was opening, and Carrie turned her head incuriously. The nurse returning to her post? But the woman who came into the room was not the nurse. Though she did not want to, automatically Carrie found herself tensing.

Berenice Nicolaides came right up to the bed and stood for a moment, just looking down at Carrie. There was a slight frown on the immaculately made-up face beneath her perfect and expensively coiffed hair.

'You look different,' she said. 'I might not have recognised you.' Her English was fluent, but the accent Greek, the tone quite deep for a woman. Her features were marked, and Carrie could see the resemblance to her son now. A 'handsome' woman, would probably be the right description. No siren. No beauty.

No bimbo.

Carrie looked at her. Two things struck her as curious. The first was that she *could* look at her—considering how at that nightmare dinner party she had just stared miserably into her plate the whole evening. The second was that the woman was not looking glacial, as she had that evening.

'I would like to talk to you,' said Alexeis's mother.

Berenice Nicolaides glanced around the shaded room. The nurse's chair was against the wall, and for a moment she looked irritated, as if a maid should be there to position the chair closer to the bed. But there was no maid in the room, so she did it herself, with ill grace. She sat herself down, crossing one leg elegantly over the other.

'I have an offer to make you,' she said. Her voice was cool, businesslike. 'I will not insult us both by prevaricating, or being evasive. My offer is this—I will pay you the sum of five million euros if you will accompany me to a very discreet clinic in Switzerland where your condition will be—dealt with.'

Carrie looked at her. She heard the words—heard them from the place where Alexeis's mother was, where the rest of the world was. But where she was not. She was somewhere else—somewhere she would not let anyone else come. Somewhere that had a high, impenetrable wall around it. A barrier that would let no feelings in—or out.

Only words.

'If you wait another few days you might save yourself such a large sum of money. Nature may well perform the service you require without payment.' Her voice was as unemotional as the other woman's offer to pay her to terminate an unwanted, unwelcome pregnancy—a personal and social disaster for Alexeis Nicolaides, her son.

'Nature is unreliable. The clinic will not be. And besides—' Berenice Nicolaides's expression changed '—I would not like you to leave empty-handed. That would not be fair. There is another reason, too. Alexeis, as you are already aware, is burdened with a sense of responsibility. He will need to be relieved of it.'

'Knowing I took your money to have an abortion will do that, I take it?' Carrie's voice still had no emotion in it.

The arched eyebrows rose. 'You are surprisingly quick to understand. Alexeis told me you are a waitress.' She said the second sentence as if it must contradict the first. Her expression changed again. She leant forward slightly. 'Will you accept my offer?'

Carrie looked at her. There was nothing in her face. Nothing at all.

Berenice Nicolaides sat back again. Her voice when she spoke next was different again. Almost conversational. 'It would be a mistake to marry my son.'

There was a moment's silence, then, 'Such a marriage would make you very unhappy. I do not speak,' she said, 'from malice. But from experience. Not mine, but that of—the woman who replaced me.' Dark eyes rested on Carrie. 'She was like you. And you, if you marry my son, will be like her. Bitterly unhappy. I would not wish her fate on you—to be a burden on a man. Alexeis will treat you well—he is not his father—but no such marriage can thrive.' The dark gaze suddenly became edged, like a knife honed to razor-sharpness. 'And if you marry my son for his money you will suffer for it, every day of your life. Do not doubt me on this! I am a bad enemy to have—do not make me one. Accept my offer or you will have cause to regret it.'

Words formed in Carrie's head. Angry, bitter words.

Aka the witch…

Cold pooled inside her. Yannis had not been lying.

Berenice Nicolaides pushed back her chair, getting to her feet. 'Well? Do you accept my offer?' Her face was glacial again, harsh and expressionless. Waiting for an answer.

Carrie gave it. The words were bitten from her. Her eyes were like basilisks.

'No. No, I will not kill my baby for five million euros. *Does that answer you?*'

Berenice Nicolaides stood still. Quite, quite still. There was nothing in her face—nothing at all.

Then she turned and left the room.

Behind her Carrie lay, trembling, her hand curving around her abdomen.

Sick at heart.

CHAPTER NINE

ALEXEIS gave up trying to talk to Carrie. Every time he asked her a question, her responses were always monosyllabic. He was not sorry to give up, he knew. Carrie was just lying there, the room still shaded, just as she had been lying there yesterday. She might not even have moved for all he knew. One thing he did know—the bleeding had not resumed. She was still pregnant.

The doctor was coming again in the afternoon. He'd told Alexeis bluntly there was nothing he could do either way, but Alexeis had asked him to come anyway. He wanted to be sure that if anything happened he would be able to tell himself afterwards that he had done everything he could to prevent it—everything he could to ensure the best level of care for Carrie.

He turned to her now and spoke. 'It's very hard,' he said, his voice halting, 'this time of waiting.'

She didn't reply.

'We just have to hope,' said Alexis.

Carrie let her eyes rest on him. She didn't speak. What could possibly be said? What could possibly be hoped for?

Nothing. Nothing could be hoped for.

I've got to get away. I've got to get away.

It was all she clung to.

I've got to get out of here.

It was imperative, essential. By any means possible, she had to get away. Escape. Escape from this house, this world. Escape from Alexeis.

Escape from the hideous fate he had planned for her.

Marriage.

Emotion savaged her again.

Does he think I'll marry him? Does he really think that?

Because she would never marry him. Never. She would give her baby away—there was nothing else to be done. Nothing! It was the only way her child could be safe—safe with a loving family of its own, safe from the fate that Alexeis threatened it with, to be raised as a duty, a responsibility, a burden...

It would crucify her to do it, but she would have to do it. There was no other way—no other way. She had gone round and round and round it in her head, the stone in her throat still, choking her...

She could not afford to raise a child on her own—would not condemn a child to the grimness of a single parent family on state support with no other family or friends to offer help or support. Even if she had the money how could she fight Alexeis, with all the wealth at his disposal? Adoption was the only way, the only hope...

The stone closed her throat, blocking everything.

Alexeis was talking again. He was always talking at her, *talking at her.* Not leaving her alone. She had to keep him out, keep him out behind the high, impenetrable wall in her head—the wall that let nothing in or out, the wall she was behind, going round and round and round...

'It is very...shaded...in here. Would you not like the blinds opened?'

'No.' Carrie's voice was expressionless. She looked at Alexeis. Her face was expressionless too. She could feel an unbearable wave of emotion trying to break into her again. She beat it down. 'I'm very tired,' she said. 'I might sleep some more.'

He nodded. 'That's probably the best,' he agreed. What else could he say?

She turned her head away again. Blotting him out of her vision.

He took his leave. Went back to the office which he was using as his base for the moment. With heavy tread, he walked up to his desk and sat down. Work, at least, absorbed his attention, his time. He was grateful for it. He reached for the mouse, clicked the screen, and got stuck in.

Alexeis went to see Carrie again at lunchtime. She was as unresponsive as she had been earlier. She said nothing in response to his dutiful enquires, just looked at him with expressionless eyes, then turned her head away to stare at the wall again. He understood why. What could she say to him? What could he say to her?

Face tight, he left her again.

Carrie heard him go. She did not want him there. She wanted to be left alone. She wanted to go on staring at the wall. It was like the wall inside her head. The wall keeping out the world. That was why she wanted the room kept shaded. So that everything on the outside would be as dark as it was on the inside.

But when the doctor came later that afternoon he had other ideas.

'You merely need rest,' he told her. 'Not to lie here as if you were in a morgue! Tomorrow you should take fresh air—I will give the necessary instructions. I will also,' he finished, 'prescribe a tonic for you. You should be on the necessary supplements for pregnancy. As well as keeping to a healthy diet.'

Carrie took the tonic and the supplements, ate the food the nurse served her though she was not hungry. Nor thirsty. Nor anything. She was glad when the doctor had gone. Alexeis went out with him, but came back a few minutes later. Carrie looked at him. The face of a stranger. That was all he was.

All he had ever been.

'I agree with the doctor,' he said bracingly. 'It isn't good for you, lying here in this gloomy room all the time. In the morning I'll have a daybed set up for you outdoors, on the terrace. Then at least you'll have a sea view.'

She didn't want a sea view. She wanted to stare at the wall, lie immobile in the dim darkness. She wanted not to be pregnant. She wanted not to be here. She wanted never to have to see Alexeis again...

I've got to get away—I've got to get away. As soon as I can—as soon as I can.

The words went round and round in her head. Round and round.

After a while, Alexeis left her again.

To get Carrie installed on a daybed on the terrace seemed to require the nurse, Alexeis, and half a dozen servants. But at last it was done. The worst had been when Alexeis had lifted her out of bed and carried her. She had frozen totally, every muscle clenched tight, eyes screwed shut.

It had been unbearable to be touched by him.

Almost as bad as talking to him. But talk she had to. Because he held the key to her escape, and she had to make him, *make him*, turn that key...

She wasn't good with words, she knew. Found them hard to select and put together. To find the things to say. It had always been hard—now it was worse. But it had to be done. She steeled herself, screwing all her resolution together.

He was sitting a little way from her, looking out to sea, shaded as she was by a large awning projecting halfway over the wide terrace. The views were spectacular—the sea a glittering blue, the sun dancing on the huge azure pool one level below, the white stone marbelline in the bright air.

It was beautiful—but she saw it as if through the far end of a telescope. Behind another wall—a glass wall this time, but just as impenetrable. It was essential that it was impenetrable. Absolutely essential.

The nurse had given her breakfast in the bedroom, but she had eaten very little. She had no appetite. The queasy feeling was back, worse than it had been before, making food even more unpalatable. There had been another dose of supplements and tonic, which she had dutifully downed. Now she had been given a cup of tea with a slice of lemon in it, from which she had taken one sip and then set aside on the table. Alexeis was drinking strong black coffee, as he always did.

Strong coffee in the morning, decaf at night. No more than three glasses of wine each evening. Fresh fruit for dessert, sometimes cheese. Still mineral water, a litre a day. Forty-five minutes in the hotel gym daily, double that at the weekends. At Portofino he swims a kilometre in the morning before breakfast, diving off the boat. He shaves twice a day and likes strong mint toothpaste that burns my mouth if I use it. He takes showers, not baths. He doesn't answer the phone during meals. He prefers fish to meat, he—

The litany marched through her head. She could not stop it. Fact after fact that she knew about Alexeis. So much she knew about him—but she had known nothing. Nothing at all…

The list mocked her. Mocked her as savagely as Alexeis's brother had done.

I've got to get away! I've got to get away, away…

'Alexeis—'

She didn't want to say his name. It was hard, grating from her. But she made herself say it. Saying it had at least made him pay attention. His body language showed it too. Turned towards her, eyes focussed on her, he waited for her to continue. Yet it was as if he were behind a thin, impenetrable sheet of glass—very far away from her. Immensely distant from her.

But then he always had been. Only she hadn't realised just how far.

'I want to go back to London,' she said. Her voice was low and strained, but she made herself speak, go on. 'I don't want to stay here any longer.'

For a moment he said nothing. Then he spoke, his tone measured.

'The doctor has said you need to continue to rest,' he answered. His voice was inexpressive, with the neutrality of distance. 'However, if you wish, as soon as…as it is possible, we can return to London. In the meantime—' he put the half-drunk coffee down on the table and got to his feet, and Carrie knew he was impatient to get away '—please follow medical advice and rest—there is nothing else to be done. For the moment we can only continue as we are, difficult though it is. I will see you again at lunchtime, but for the moment I hope you will excuse me. I have to get some work done.'

He gave her a constrained, perfunctory smile, and headed off. Carrie watched him go, nails digging into the palm of her hand.

She couldn't bear to be here! Couldn't bear it! Every fibre of her body screamed at her to go, run, get away, *away*, as fast and as far as she could. The urgency of it overwhelmed her.

But she was trapped here. Trapped in this villa whose luxury mocked her, punished her…

I used to revel in the luxury—in the life he gave me! Revelled in it all! And all along...

Shame and guilt flushed through her like acid—and bitter, bitter self-disgust.

Her gaze travelled bleakly out over the view in front of her. Brilliant sunlight dancing on an azure sea, the pristine crescent of beach curving by the edge of the waves. She gazed blankly down. Not wanting to see it. She didn't want to be here. She wanted to be back in the bedroom, the blinds drawn, with the blank wall to stare at. The wall inside her head keeping her safe... But she had been brought out here, into the brightness, into the warmth and the sunshine. With all the world around her. Forcing her to see it. Forcing her to look.

And as she looked at the image of the pristine beach, the lapping, azure sea, as she felt the fresh air on her face, the sunlight on her skin, she felt as if deep, deep inside her something was cracking—cracking with long, spidery threads. Breaking and piercing, fracturing.

She tried to stop it, tried to halt it, tried to hold it back, hold it up. Tried frantically, desperately, to shore it up again.

But it was crumbling, crumbling and breaking, and she couldn't stop it. She couldn't, she couldn't...

And then it came. Like a huge, unstoppable wave. Crushing down the wall, sweeping it aside, pouring past, taking her over, overwhelming her, overpowering her...

In a last, final act of desperation, she shut her eyes. Screwed them shut, covered them with her hands to keep it out...*out*...

But it was there. Vivid. Scoring into her retinas. And she couldn't stop it, she couldn't stop it...

Alexeis down there on the beach. Laughing. Lifting up a child—a child who laughed with him in glee. And beside

Alexeis someone else. A woman with long blonde hair, her face alight with love and happiness—holding out her arms to her child, to Alexeis...

And Alexeis folded her to him, to their child...

She cried out, a muffled cry, tearing open her eyes, making herself, *forcing* herself, to stare down at the deserted beach. No one was there. It was as it had been before. Empty. Bare.

Her vision blurred. Smeared. Tears filled her eyes. With a choke of misery she turned her head away, into her pillow.

And grief engulfed her for what could never, never be.

Her hand stole over her abdomen. Protective. Despairing.

Because how could she hope for what was nothing more than a fantasy—a fantasy as unreal, as cruel, as the one she had just had ripped from her? A fantasy a thousand times less real, a thousand times more cruel...a fantasy of the impossible.

Slowly, her hand slipped to her side.

Slowly, brick by brick, she rebuilt the wall, shutting out the world. Shutting out the light. Shutting out cruel, impossible hope. Finally facing reality.

She went back to waiting.

All I can do is wait—wait to lose my child. One way or the other...

The agony of it was unbearable.

But bear it she must.

Alexeis stared at the computer screen. He had told Carrie he had to get some work done, but he had only said that to get away from her. After all, it was what she wanted too. She couldn't have made it clearer. Not speaking to him, turning her head away—freezing like a statue when he'd picked her up.

Frustration bit in him. Hell, he was doing his best! He was trying to be as supportive, as protective as he could, in a situation that neither of them could possibly have wanted! He was prepared to marry her, to do the decent thing, take responsibility for the situation. What more could he do?

Restlessly, he pushed his chair back, walked to the French window that opened on to the upper terrace, stepped out into the fresh air.

The weather was heating up. The hot Greek summer was nearly on them. His hands closed down over the sun-warmed stone of the balustrade and he gazed unseeingly around him. It was all so familiar. He'd spent summers here as a child, whilst his mother and father had argued bitterly over the baby that had destroyed their marriage.

He shifted his weight from one foot to the other. Remembering the past wasn't conducive to happiness. Yannis too had had a tormented childhood, thanks to their mutual father. Yannis had been a possession, nothing more. Unlike Berenice Nicolaides, Yannis's mother had held no power, had been unable to afford expensive lawyers. So when she'd fled a marriage that had proved nothing but misery for her her son had simply been taken from her…

Familiar loathing welled in Alexeis. Did his father possess a single redeeming feature?

Not when it came to his family.

Or his children.

Alexeis's expression hardened. Who would want to bring yet more children into a family like his?

But that was exactly what he'd done. Carelessly, accidentally, unintentionally. It didn't matter. If a child were born then it would be as real as his own brother was real.

Into his head his mother's voice sounded. An honourable man, she had called him. His mouth twisted. Honourable? Honourable enough to be prepared to marry a woman he hardly knew to legitimise a child that neither had planned for?

Was that honour? Was that 'doing the decent thing'? The words mocked him.

But what else can I do? It's all I can do! There's nothing else I can do!

His hands pressed down over the balustrade. Another voice sounded in his head. A voice he tried to blank out. A voice that would not be silenced.

Isn't there? Isn't there something else you can do? You can stop behaving like a spoilt, selfish playboy, pitying yourself because your comfortable, familiar bachelor existence is under threat! Stop feeling virtuous because you're prepared to accept your responsibilities, do the decent thing...

Angrily, he tried to silence the voice, but it would not be silenced.

You enjoy an existence privileged beyond the dreams of millions! And you dare to pity yourself! You talk about what else you can do, when it's staring you in the face! It's not about doing the decent thing!

But doing the right thing.

Being the father that yours never was. A father worthy of his child.

And out of nowhere the resolution came to him. Came sweeping in like a tide, powerful and overwhelming. No, he hadn't asked for this. No, he had not welcomed it. But fate had made it so, and he would not betray his child by wishing it unborn, uncreated. Emotion swept through him again. Fierce and protective. Strong and cherishing.

I'll be the best father it is in my power to be! You will be safe with me—safe and loved.

And I will never, never wish you lost to me—

He gazed out over the balustrade, down to the beach below. A beach he'd played on as a child.

And my child will too.

And Carrie will be there, beside me. She will be a loving mother—gentle and kind and loving. What does it matter if she isn't 'suitable' to be the wife of a Nicolaides? I will let no one sneer at her—no one mock her! Her limitations are not her fault. She is not to blame for them.

His mouth tightened. Would he rather have had Marissa pregnant with his child? Or Adrianna? Rejection, instant and powerful, speared through him.

Memory sifted in him from long, long ago. He could scarcely remember Yannis's mother from when she had been his nursemaid, but he could remember a softness about her, a gentleness. When he had fallen, she'd picked him up and hugged him. She'd sat him on her lap and sung funny English nursery rhymes to him, songs that had clapping games in them, and she had laughed and smiled.

He had missed her when she'd gone…

Carrie will be like her—warm and loving, gentle and caring. What else does a child need?

And as for himself—

Well, as a mother to his child, he would have no complaints over Carrie. As a woman for his bed—again, he could hardly complain. And as a wife by his side, through the long years to come—?

His mind sheered away. He would cope with it when it happened. Until then there was nothing to do but wait. His future held in the balance of a fate he could not control.

That night, the waiting ended. Carrie started to bleed. This time she did not stop.

Alexeis was outside her bedroom. Inside was the doctor, summoned urgently, and the nurse on constant duty, who had raised the alarm. Alexeis did not go in. Carrie did not want him in the room, the doctor had informed him, his expression grave. He had told him there was nothing he could do. There was nothing anyone could do.

Alexeis sat, his face stark, until the doctor came out again. His face was graver yet. Alexeis looked at him, his expression haggard.

'I should go to her,' he said after a moment.

The doctor shook his head. 'I have given her a sedative and painkillers. She will need to sleep for quite some time.' He frowned slightly. 'I am sorry,' he said again. He gave a heavy sigh. 'Nature finds her own way, and sometimes…' he paused '…sometimes it is for the best.'

He took his leave, saying he would return when his patient was awake again.

Alexeis stood in the villa hallway, quite immobile. Then, forcing himself, he went to Carrie's room. The nurse was there, the low light beside her chair the only illumination. She made to speak, but Alexeis silenced her with a hand. He went to look at Carrie.

Lines were etched deep into her face, and her brow sweated, her hair matted. Alexeis stood for some time, looking down at her. She did not stir, the rise and fall of her chest hardly discernible. Her lips were slightly parted, the air scarcely passing between them.

He looked down at her and did not know what to feel. Knew only that the balance of his life had changed. And that his unborn child had paid the price for it.

Guilt skewered through him.

There should have been something I could have done. There should have been something—anything! Anything!

But it was over now. Finished.

He went on gazing down at Carrie's unconscious form. Emotion, inchoate and shapeless, heaved within him. After a while he walked away, giving instructions to the nurse that he be called when she woke.

The past had come back to him. The future had turned back into the past.

But at a price that was—abhorrent.

Carrie awoke to full and instant consciousness. Whatever the doctor had injected into her, it had not blocked memory. Or vision.

Alexeis was there. His tall figure was silhouetted against the slatted blinds through which shards of sunshine were knifing. He didn't say anything, and he seemed tense, remote. A stranger.

But that was all he ever had been.

A stranger who had got her pregnant by accident. A pregnancy that was now no more.

She saw him steeling himself, then he spoke. 'Carrie—' his voice was heavy '—I am so very, very sorry.'

She heard the words, let them hang in the air. Let them hang like the lies they were. Alexeis was not sorry—how could he be? How could he be sorry that his bimbo tart wasn't pregnant any more? He was going through the expected motions, that was all—just as he had when he'd nobly offered to marry her.

God, he must be thanking heaven and all the saints for this reprieve! Thinking himself such a lucky, lucky man!

Like a scorpion inside her, the vicious thoughts stung and bit. But she did not turn them into words. Why should she? Why should she say anything to Alexeis ever again?

She turned her head away, back to staring at the wall.

'Carrie—'

He had taken her hand. She jerked it away. He did not try to take it again.

'Carrie, I— Please, look at me, talk to me—'

But loathing filled her heart. And then something far worse than loathing.

Emptiness.

For a while Alexeis just went on standing there, looking down at her averted face. Helpless frustration filled him. He wanted to comfort her, but how? How could he comfort her? She was still shutting him out, turning away from him.

I've got to get her away from here. Away from the misery and the memory.

His brow furrowed. The only thing she had said to him was that she wanted to go back to London. He had said yes, of course—because he had not wanted to have any kind of confrontation with her. But the very last thing he would do was take her back to London—

She needed rest, recuperation and recovery. Physical and emotional.

He stood staring down at her. He felt hollow, disoriented, as if he could not believe what had happened, that something that had been about to change his life for ever was now—over. Finished. Never to be. It was the same shock he'd felt when the doctor had told him why Carrie had collapsed. There was a blankness, a nullity, all through him, and his mind would not think, would not operate.

Was it the same for her? Compunction struck him. It must be a hundred times worse for her! She had gone through the physical experience of being pregnant, of bleeding, with the torment of not knowing whether her baby would live or die. And now it was all over. All over.

The strange, dead feeling of blankness thickened in him. *We've got to get away—*

The impulse was more urgent now, more imperative.

Sardinia—we'll just go to Sardinia. I'll take her there, the way I planned, before…

An image formed in his mind—Carrie and him, relaxing at the luxury hotel he would take her to, the scent of pine trees, the azure of a personal pool, soft music playing, discreet and private, just the two of them. A sanctuary for them both.

She would rest there, recover.

Yes, that was what he'd do. Take her to Sardinia. Far, far away from here. From what had happened.

The bleak hollowness inside him seemed to intensify. On an impulse he reached his hand out—not to try and take hers again, but just to touch her hair. As he grazed one pale strand she flinched away from him, and he drew his hand back sharply. Frustration welled in him again. And more than frustration. An emotion he did not recognise, could not name. He wanted to touch her again, but he made himself hold back. There was nothing he could do yet. No comfort to give—or take. She needed time. And time was what he would give her.

He had to remove her from this place that had once again been the scene of unhappiness, one more twist in the knotted rope that bound his family.

He left the room, instructing the nurse that Carrie was to have every care, and that he was to be called if there was the slightest need whatsoever. Then he went back to his office, back to the oblivion of work, the blank hollow still deep inside him.

CHAPTER TEN

HE GAVE Carrie two days to herself, leaving her entirely to the nurse and to the doctor, whom he summoned to check her over yet again, despite being told it was not necessary. The doctor was blunt.

'I do not discount her trauma, but she must not be allowed to sink into depression. I can prescribe pills, but best would be a change of scene. Somewhere where she can recover fully. She may not want to—may want only to go on lying in that darkened room of hers, wishing for something that can never now be. But it is not good for her. Though it will take time, move on she must.'

Alexeis nodded, glad to have the doctor back up what he himself wanted.

'When will she be up to travelling?'

'She is young and strong. If the journey is not arduous, I would say at any time.'

It was what he wanted to hear. 'Thank you,' he said.

The doctor picked up his bag again. 'And in the meantime get her out of that damn morgue of a room! She needs light and fresh air. Ignore any protestations. It will be the depression speaking, not herself.'

He took his leave, and Alexeis gave the staff the necessary

instructions. He gave her time to become settled back on the daybed on the terrace, under the awning, then he steeled himself to go out.

As he walked along the terrace towards her, he felt a harrowing sense of *déjà vu* come over him. The last time he had seen her there, she had still been carrying his child.

Now—

Now he had to try and get her to move forward, into a different future from the one that might have been.

He came up to her.

She must have heard him, but she did not change her position. She was looking out to sea. In the far distance Alexeis could just make out a white sail. Emotion twisted in him. How short a space ago had he looked out to sea with a maelstrom of thoughts in his head… That future was gone.

He straightened his shoulders. Now it was the present he had to mend. To heal.

He sat himself down on a chair by the table set within convenient reach of her, so she could sip from the restorative tonic that the doctor had prescribed her. That it was untouched did not surprise him. She was paler than ever. Frailer than ever. He felt emotion twist in him again.

'Carrie—'

How many times had he said her name, only to have her not respond, avert her head? But now, as he spoke, she turned towards him.

'When am I going back to London?' she said. Her voice was very composed. Very calm.

And as distant as if she had been a thousand miles away.

Alexeis frowned. 'London?' he echoed blankly.

Surely she did not think he was about to throw her out? Send her packing? He must reassure her immediately.

'Carrie, there is no question of you going to London,' he

began. 'What I propose, and the doctor agrees with me, is that we go somewhere you can recuperate fully, recover from your ordeal, the terrible trauma you have undergone. We shall go to Sardinia, as we originally planned. There you can rest, convalesce—'

He broke off. Carrie was staring at him, her eyes distended, huge in her face, which seemed painfully thin suddenly, stark and strained, her beautiful hair lank and lustreless. Then, as if a switch had been thrown, she lurched to her feet, rigid in every limb but swaying, as if she had no more substance than silk. Instinctively, Alexeis jerked upright, his hands going out to catch her. His hands caught her shoulders to stabilise her.

Her reaction was violent. She threw him off, moving backwards against the balustrade.

'Don't *touch* me! I can't bear you to touch me!'

Shock etched through Alexeis again. 'Carrie—what—?'

'Oh, God—you sit there and talk about going to Sardinia as though nothing has happened!'

Alexeis's hands lifted in instant denial. 'No—that isn't it! That's not it at all—Carrie, please. Listen to me! What's happened has been terrible, but—'

She wouldn't let him finish. Her face was contorted. Emotion was tearing through her—emotion that had been banked, and which now wouldn't stop pouring, tearing through her.

'Terrible? Oh, God, yes, terrible! Terrible that I got pregnant. Terrible that you had to face the hideous ordeal of offering to marry me! Well, don't worry. You'd never have had to go through with it—I'd have given the child up for adoption!'

'*What?*'

Her eyes flashed, chest heaving with emotion. 'Do you

think I'd wish *any* child on your disgusting family? Do you think I'd let a child have *anything* to do with a family where its own grandmother wanted it aborted?'

'What are you saying? What the hell are you saying, Carrie?'

Her face contorted again. 'Your mother came to me and offered me five million euros to get rid of the baby!'

Alexeis's face paled. 'No. No—that cannot be. It can't.'

Fury twisted her features. 'Do you think I was deaf when she spoke to me? When she warned me off marrying you? When she told me she'd make sure I was sorry if I dared to marry you?'

'*When*—when did she say this to you?' Alexeis's blood was starting to run cold. In his head he heard his mother's words, so apparently innocuous, so devoted. '*I will always guard your interests...everything I do is for you.*'

'When? When she paid me a little visit. Forced herself to talk to her precious son's little tart he'd installed in her very own tart's boudoir. The same beach house that your father installed his own mistress in! The tart he'd specially lined up for the sole purpose of showing his mother what kind of woman he preferred and not to bother to keep trying to marry him off!'

Alexeis's face was a mask. How in God's name had Carrie come up with this? Her eyes were burning, her face contorted.

'And I hadn't a clue—not a clue! But then why should I have? I was only a stupid little bimbo, too thick to know what was going on! A stupid, thick little bimbo that your disgusting brother had to explain everything to in vivid, living colour, so my single brain cell could grasp it!'

Alexeis jerked.

'*Yannis?* Yannis told you these things?'

'Yes, Yannis!'

'*When*—when did he tell you these things?' Alexeis's voice was tight with anger.

'That morning—the morning I collapsed!'

His face darkened. So that damn white sail he'd seen had been sailing away from the beach—after Yannis had done his poisonous damage…

Carrie was still spitting out her venom. 'He swanned in the morning after you paraded me like an idiot at your mother's dinner table! Telling me *all* about it! Telling me just why you'd gone slumming and picked up a bimbo for your bed! Telling me *all* about your vile, vile family!'

An expletive broke from Alexeis, angry and vocal.

'*Christos*, what Yannis says isn't worth the air it takes to say it! How could you pay the slightest attention to him?'

'Because what he said was *true*, that's why! I let you pick me up off the street and I was in your bed that same night! And I let you give me expensive clothes and stay in posh hotels and wear diamond jewellery. I'm *exactly* what your brother called me! I'm a stupid, brainless little bimbo— nothing but airhead arm-candy. And what I was stupid enough, brainless enough, to think *glamorous* and *thrilling* and *romantic* was just tacky and cheap and sordid. Having sex with you because it came with designer clothes and yachts and champagne and flying first class and on private jets and helicopters and—'

Alexeis slashed his hand through the air, negating what was pouring from her.

'It wasn't like that!' There was anger in his voice. Absolute rejection.

'It was *exactly* like that!' Her voice was cracking as she cried back at him. She looked at him, her skin stretched tight across her bones. 'I always knew I couldn't really cope with all the people you know. I don't know anything about art, or politics, or theatre, or literature, or grand opera. Yes, I know I'm not very good at conversation, and I don't speak any foreign languages, but I never actually thought…I never actually thought that you just saw me as some kind of tart.' Another ragged intake of breath scissored through her lungs. 'Which just goes to show how incredibly, incredibly stupid I am.'

Alexeis drew a breath. It was like a razor in his lungs. Somehow, *somehow*, he had to…had to…

What? What had he got to do? Cold poured down his spine. The world had just imploded in his face.

Desperately he tried to find the words he needed.

'Carrie, I've never thought of you in that way. Never! You must believe me. You must! Yes, I admit I saw an opportunity to convince my mother to stop trying to matchmake by taking you to dinner as my partner. But I thought…' His voice went flat suddenly, and he found he did not want to look her in the eyes. 'I thought you wouldn't notice there was a…a hidden agenda. I knew you wouldn't meet any of those people again, so what did it matter what they thought of you?'

For a moment she said nothing, then, with a quietness that cut the air like a scalpel, she said, 'And it didn't matter what *you* thought of me, either, did it? Or what I was. Because I was just what you wanted. Someone pretty and eager and impressionable and willing in bed?'

'Carrie, just because you're not the intellectual type, it doesn't mean—' He broke off. 'Look, don't put yourself down—' He broke off again. Whatever he said, however he said it, it was impossible to say. But one thing he *had* to say—however unpalatable.

'I never intended you to realise why I'd brought you for dinner that night,' he said starkly. 'It was all supposed to—' he took a difficult breath '—to go over your head.'

'Because I'm a bimbo and wouldn't be expected to notice?' Her eyes were unblinking.

'Carrie, I—'

'But you are right. That's exactly the word for me.'

Alexeis's hand slashed through the air again. 'No! I won't let you say that about yourself! I enjoyed giving you a taste of a world you had never experienced. I enjoyed seeing how much pleasure you took in drinking champagne and flying first class. I was happy to indulge you, and buy you beautiful clothes to make you even more beautiful than you are!'

'And you did this out of the kindness of your heart? If I had been plain as an old boot you'd still have indulged me? Taken me first class and put diamonds around my neck?' She shook her head. 'No, you did it because you wanted to have sex with me. That's what you were getting out of it. While I was getting my champagne, and my designer wardrobe. That's what makes me a tart. Stupidity isn't a crime—but what I did was. I blinded myself to what I was doing because I didn't want to see it that way. I wanted to see the romance, not the reality.'

A bitter look crossed her face suddenly. 'I deluded myself that I wasn't like silly Madame Butterfly, but that's just what I was—a geisha girl all along. Nothing more than that.' Her voice became flat again. 'But at least I was spared her fate—spared bearing a child to a man I meant nothing to.' Unconsciously, her fingers fluttered over her abdomen. Then they dropped uselessly to her side. There was nothing left to protect.

Nothing left to do but go.

The sunlight dazzling all around mocked her, punished her. She was empty—empty of everything.

There was silence between them. What more could be said? Nothing. Nothing at all.

Then Alexeis spoke. 'I'll arrange for you to go back to London tomorrow,' he said. His voice was completely flat.

* * *

He didn't see her again before she left. He told himself, staring into his computer screen, that it was for her sake. But he knew it wasn't true.

He worked late, obliterating his mind with business matters—of which there were many. He made sure of it. He worked non-stop, living on black coffee and trays of food, until at length his eyes were gritty from screen work and there was no one left around the world he hadn't teleconferenced with. Then and only then was he forced out from his office.

The villa seemed very quiet now Carrie had left.

There was an emptiness that was gaping.

He walked out onto the terrace. Further along it opened out into a wide paved area, large enough to take a twenty-foot dining table, should his mother wish to dine *al fresco* under the stars. Mostly, however, she preferred to dine indoors, as she had the evening he'd brought Carrie to the villa.

He stopped short.

In his mind's eye he saw the table ringed with people, his mother's houseguests, and his mother at its head. Anastasia Savarkos was on her right, looking austerely elegant in the high-necked olive-green evening gown, her dark hair drawn back from her face, pearls discreetly at her ears, her make-up minimal and subtle. Her entire image a total contrast to that of the girl sitting beside him.

He saw again the tempting swell of Carrie's breasts above the low-cut gown, her bare shoulders and back creamy and exposed, her long blonde hair flowing wantonly in tousled locks, her eyes huge with make-up, her mouth rich and bee-stung from his kiss. Sitting beside him saying nothing, because she had nothing to say, because they were all speaking Greek around her and no one wanted to talk to her, to acknowledge her existence, cutting her dead.

His jaw tightened and he turned away, heading down a flight of steps that led to a lower-level terrace.

She wasn't supposed to know why I'd brought her there! She was supposed to be oblivious to it!

Oblivious to the fact that he'd deliberately wanted her to look like the kind of woman who kept a man from marriage, whose function in his life was to warm his bed, provide his sexual pleasures.

'You paraded me like a tart!'

Her brutal, vicious words seared in his memory.

An emotion stabbed that was alien to him. That he'd never felt before. That for a timeless, twisted moment he could not put a name to. Then its name came to him, knifing through him.

Shame.

Shame at what he had done.

I made her look exactly what she said! Knowingly, deliberately! I used her, without any thought, for my own ends. Telling myself that as she would never find out it didn't matter that I did so.

The night took him in as he stepped out onto the dark lower terrace, only the unearthly glow of the pool lights piercing the darkness around him.

Telling myself that since she would never know any of the people there it didn't matter—it didn't matter what they thought of her.

More words she'd thrown at him came back to him. Even more stabbing.

'And it didn't matter what you thought of me, either, did it? Or what I was. Because I was just what you wanted. Someone pretty and eager and impressionable and willing in bed.'

But he *hadn't* thought of her as a bimbo! Or a tart! Those

vile, vicious words were not his—they were Yannis's, poisoning Carrie's mind. And what the *hell* had Yannis been playing at, to accost Carrie the way he had? Stirring up trouble for its own sake! Daring to speak so offensively to Carrie, calling her those cruel, crude, ugly names!

I never thought of her like that—never!

His expression changed. He could acquit himself of that charge—his conscience was clear on that score. Yannis might think of women like that, but he never would. And not Carrie! *Not Carrie!*

But into his head wound more words. Uncomfortable, probing.

So she was just pretty and eager and willing in bed—was that it? Was that the sum total of her charms for you?

More memories—memories that carried a different emotion. One that was worse to feel.

Her eyes widening in wonder as I took her to places she'd never dreamt of experiencing. Getting a kick from wearing a fantastic evening gown, drinking vintage champagne. Like a kid let loose in a toy store...

Had that been making a tart of her? A woman who traded sex for luxury?

Again he fought back against the accusation.

It didn't feel that way! Money never came into it. And she never angled for anything, never played the coquette. It never once felt like I was rewarding her for having sex with me.

And as for saying if he hadn't found her sexually desirable, he wouldn't have lavished luxury on her—well, if he hadn't found her sexually desirable he wouldn't have been interested in her in the first place! What was the crime in desiring her? He'd wanted her—he'd taken her with him. She'd shared his luxurious lifestyle because that was the lifestyle that was natural to him.

He gazed bleakly out over the terraces and gardens. The air was rich with the sound of cicadas and the scent of flowers, the sound of the water lapping the shore. Luxurious and beautiful.

Was that how it had been with Carrie? She supplied the beauty and he supplied the luxury? Was that why she'd stayed with him? Had that been his sole appeal for her?

His face tightened. Certainty, absolute and unilateral, filled him.

No. Categorically, unequivocally, no. No hesitation, no doubt. Nothing. Nothing but knowing that if they'd both been in rags, in a hovel, Carrie would still have melted into his arms, still come to shuddering ecstasy in his embrace, still clung to him, trembling with desire, while he caressed her silken body towards fulfilment.

Emotion knifed him.

Powerful, piercing.

Unbearable.

Knifing through his head on the blade of memory was Carrie, cradled against him, all passion spent, as he gently stroked her hair, her breath warm on his bare skin, finding peace after satiation. Rest after the tumult of the flesh. Quietness after a climax of the senses.

Carrie—

Her name, that was all, sounding in his head. All he had left of her…

'Missing her?'

The voice came out of nowhere, from the pool of darkness at the far end of the terrace. A familiar voice, and one he did not want to hear. He seldom did, and now even more so. Yannis strolled out of the darkness. His voice was taunting, grating.

'What the hell are you doing here?' Alexeis's voice was terse, demanding. A new emotion was taking over, fuelled by a rush of adrenaline that had come the moment he'd heard his brother's taunting voice. An emotion that tensed and coiled in every muscle of his body.

'Don't tell me I'm trespassing?' Yannis responded drawlingly. 'Going to get Security to throw me out, back to my own humble neck of the woods? And to think I just thought you might like some company—seeing as how you're on your lonesome tonight. I'm sorry you are—if only for the novelty value of seeing you with a real live bimbo!' His eyes glinted in the dim light. 'Pity you packed the bimbo off—I'd have been happy to take her off your hands. Your leftovers don't normally appeal to me, but I'd have made an exception for this one. She was a real peach! OK, so she was as thick as clotted cream, but twice as tasty. I'd have lapped her up, no problem!'

The coiling tension in Alexeis's muscles snapped. His fist impacted with Yannis's jaw, sending him reeling back against the balustrade.

'What the—?'

Yannis's hand flew to his jaw. He straightened, his hand rubbing the bruised flesh.

'Well, well,' he said slowly. There was something different in his voice. 'Is this for real? Alexeis Nicolaides, who disposes of women like they're used tissues, defending a maiden's honour ? So what's with the hottie bimbo that you have to take your fist to me?'

Alexeis reached forward, his hand clamping like steel over Yannis's shoulder. His face was twisted with fury.

'You keep your foul mouth shut about her, Yannis. You've done enough damage as it is! What the hell did you think you were playing at—telling her all that garbage, poisoning her mind?'

Yannis's eyes lasered into his brother's. 'Garbage? It was

the truth! You brought her here to put paid to the witch's plans for you and Anastasia Savarkos—do you want to deny it?'

'She didn't need to know!' snarled Alexeis.

Anger was roiling in him, fuelled by the adrenaline surging round his over-tired, over-tensed body. He wanted to smash his fist into Yannis's face again, wanted to pulverise him for what he'd said to Carrie. He wasn't fit to mention her name, let alone the filth he was spouting about her now!

His brother gave a bark of harsh laughter. 'Oh, no—much better if she knows what she's being set up for! Then it's job done, off you go, sweetheart. Thanks for all the hot sex, but I'm sure I've made it worth your while—'

Alexeis moved to hit him again.

But this time Yannis's hand whipped up, stopping Alexeis's fist. For a moment both men silently opposed each other's strength. Alexeis's fist drove forward, meeting an immovable force. Their faces were stark with enmity. Then, abruptly, Alexeis dropped his fist and stood back.

'You say one more word—one word,' he spelt out, his eyes boring like steel drills into Yannis's, 'about her, and I will beat you to a pulp.' He took a harsh, razored breath. 'Carrie was pregnant. I didn't know. Nor did she. She collapsed right after you'd spilled your filth into her ears. She miscarried three days ago.'

There was silence—complete and absolute. Only the lap of the water on the beach and the cicadas in the vegetation could be heard.

Then, slowly, Yannis spoke. His voice different.

'Oh, hell.' It was all he said.

It seemed to Alexeis, suddenly, that it was a very good word—it covered everything that had happened.

'She went home because she wanted to,' he said. 'She didn't want to be with me any more. Not after—everything.'

He let the last word stand for itself. He didn't want to spell it out. His brother had done a good enough job on that.

He turned his head, looking out to sea. He'd done a lot of that in these last hellish days. A lot of turning away, looking away.

'What do I say?' said Yannis, in a voice Alexeis did not associate with his brother. It was careful—strangely blank. 'Do I say that's harsh? Do I say if you want someone to get drunk with, I'm your man? Or do I say…' his voice changed again, dropping in pitch '…it could have been worse. She might have stayed pregnant.'

Alexeis looked back at him. The present and the past co-alesced yet again, dragging the poisoned eddies of the past into the turbid, swirling waters of the present.

'The way your mother did?'

'Got it in one,' said Yannis. There was a drawl in his voice again. 'If she'd miscarried she'd have been chucked out the same day—and she'd have had a chance of a normal life. Instead she had to marry our esteemed father. Having been nothing to him but his convenient source of handy sex—his bimbo mistress, as all the world knew—now she was rolled out as Mrs Aristides Nicolaides the second.'

His eyes were on Alexeis, and Alexeis could feel the barb in them. It made him want to take a slug at Yannis again, even though this time it would not have been justified. Instead, in a voice as dry as paper, he said, 'Well, in that respect history was not about to repeat itself. Carrie informed me she had no intention of marrying me, and said she was going to have the baby adopted.'

Something shifted in Yannis's blue eyes. He gave a soft whistle. 'What brought that on?'

Alexeis's mouth thinned. 'You did,' he said brutally. 'Your enlightening little chat with her down by the beach house.'

Yannis held up his hands. 'Uh-uh—don't try and lay it on

me! I opened her eyes, that's all! Told it like it was! She should thank me!' There was a bite in his voice, aggression only just beneath the surface.

'Strangely,' ground out Alexeis, 'gratitude is not the emotion she harbours for you, brother mine. And nor do I!'

Yannis rubbed at his jaw reflectively. 'Yeah, I noticed. So maybe, "brother mine—"' he echoed the phrase with deliberate taunting '—you might feel grateful to me for this, then. Tell me—that foxy diva you ran round with in Milan last year, with the temper and personality of a ferret on heat, and that one in London, the slinky brunette with the lush lips who thought the sun shone out of her own toned little backside—' He stopped.

'Yes?' said Alexeis impatiently. Why the hell was Yannis bringing up Adrianna and Marissa?

'I'm waiting,' said Yannis.

'You're what?' Alexeis's brows snapped together.

'I'm waiting,' said Yannis, his eyes holding his brother's, 'for you to slug me.'

'Slug you?' said Alexeis blankly. 'What for?'

'What made them so different,' Yannis went on, his eyes never leaving Alexeis's, 'from the hot-sex blonde bimbo you brought here?'

Then Alexeis hit him. 'I *said*,' he snarled, 'don't *ever* foulmouth Carrie again!'

His brother staggered back exaggeratedly, rubbing his jaw with a slow, deliberate action. He smiled before he spoke. 'Just as I thought. I foul-mouthed two women you picked for sex, and it didn't even register. But I say one word about Carrie and you slug me faster than I can say her name.'

He took another step backwards, still rubbing at his twice-bruised jaw.

'Time for me to beat it, before you get a taste for blood!

Just think about it will you? And when you've thought about it…' he half turned, pausing as he did so '…do something about it. We may be the family from hell—but we don't have to stay that way. Just hold that thought, OK?'

Then he was gone, slipping back into the night he'd come out of.

Leaving Alexeis behind, with a raised heart-rate, stinging knuckles, and a brain in tumult. And thoughts going round in his head he didn't want to think.

Feelings he did not want to feel.

CHAPTER ELEVEN

CARRIE stirred, glad to awake from heavy, humid sleep. It was the noise of traffic that woke her in the mornings—buses rumbling down the busy road in Paddington in the early hours. She wasn't used to it any more. Nor was she used to sleeping, living and eating in a single room, where the ugly-patterned wallpaper was peeling off in the corners, the carpet needed to go on a rubbish tip, and the electricity ran on a meter.

I've been spoilt. Spoilt by luxury.

The thought shamed her.

Added itself to the mountain of shame she already felt. To the shame of what she had done, what she had been, that had burst from her like an infected wound that last hideous morning. It felt as though it had been lanced from the depths inside her, where it had been seeping, day after day, as she had lain in bed at the villa, waiting to see whether the frail, fragile life growing within her would cling to existence.

Or be a sacrifice to free her from a man who'd got his mistress pregnant and was steeling himself to marry her.

Well, the sacrifice had been made, and she was free. But the price paid crushed guiltily down on her head and she knew she would never, never be free of it.

Yet if the baby had lived all she could have offered it was being given to another family—not even being looked after by herself, its own mother…

Guilt stabbed her from every side. Guilt that she had been complicit in being what she knew she had been to Alexeis, and yet had denied the sordid reality of it. Guilt that she had got pregnant and miscarried—and guilt, burning like acid on her skin, that she had to face knowing that it was better for such a child never to have been born…

But with the guilt and shame also came memories that wound clinging tentacles in her mind, taunting her with images she could not resist or turn off. A hundred, thousand memories—like treacherous ghosts she wanted to banish, to ban, but could not! They came and came, tormenting and clinging to her… Alexeis looking at her, those lambent, long-lashed eyes sweeping over her, rendering her boneless and weak. Alexeis reaching for her, his hands curving posses-sively around her waist, drawing her to him in desire, cradling her against him, hushing her softly, his hand stroking down the fall of her hair in the trembling aftermath of passion. Alexeis lying in her embrace, his face in repose, as she gazed, wonderingly, at the perfection of his features. Alexeis—always Alexeis. Image after image. Memory after memory. By day and by night, but especially—tormenting her the most—at night. In her dreams. Her mind wanted to forget—her dreams did not.

Three nights since she had come back to London, and each one had brought those dreams. Dreams that shamed her. That pulled tighter the noose of guilt around her throat. That showed her just how low she had sunk.

I know what I did—I know what I was to him! So how can I still have dreams like that—memories like that? How can I?

And worst of all was the realisation that if her dreams stopped, then there would be in their place emptiness.

An emptiness like a terrifying chasm inside her. An emptiness to make her want to weep, cry out, rail at the heavens, at fate, at nature, at whatever it was that had convulsed her womb. She heard again—again and again—the doctor's pitying voice—*'My dear, it is nature's way... There was something wrong... It is kinder that it happens now...'*

And worst—worst of all—the chill, excoriating fear within her.

It was my punishment.

I did not deserve my baby because I conceived it with such a man, in such a way, and so it was taken from me.

The weight of it bowed and crushed her down.

And yet she knew she had to accept what had happened. There was no alternative. Her baby was gone. Alexeis was gone. The former would cause her grief for ever, she knew, but the latter—oh, the latter she must only be glad of. *Must* be glad of.

What else should I be but glad? Glad to have my eyes opened to the truth about it.

But gladness was not something she felt.

She steeled herself. It didn't matter what she did or didn't feel. Slowly, painfully, she had to go on with her life. The harsh reality of having once again to make ends meet was something she welcomed. It soaked up her time, her energy and her mind. And with every day that passed, the past was getting further away.

At least she still had her bedsit, poky as it was. The rent had been paid in advance, before she'd left London in a haze, a daze of dazzled wonder, and again while she was with Alexeis in America. But the next payment was due, and unless she wanted to find herself on the streets she had to earn money to make it.

She'd gone down to the job agency the day after arriving back in London, never for a single moment regretting that she had not cashed the cheque that had been enclosed with her airline ticket.

'To tide you over,' Alexeis had written. But she hadn't taken it. She had torn it up. She had lived off Alexeis quite long enough…earning her keep in his bed. Now she would earn honestly again. So what if the work were boring and tedious and poorly paid? It was honest labour—and it would not be necessary for ever. She just had to get through to the end of the summer, that was all. That was her horizon. Her future.

I'll be over him by then. He'll be nothing more than an ugly memory. And by then the dreams will have stopped…

But until then she was temporary receptionist by day and a waitress again by night. They were boring jobs, and it was tiring, working from morning till late, but she had no alternative. At least the work, tedious and tiring as it was, kept her busy. But it was grim, and dreary, and unrelenting, and London in summer mocked her, showing blue skies and a warm sun imprisoned in a city that imprisoned her too, between the crowds and the noise and pollution, the traffic and non-stop rushing.

A bone-white terrace, gleaming beneath a brilliant sun, an azure sea—

She banished the image, the memory, conjuring others to take its place. The bedroom of the beach house—a tart's boudoir. The dining room in the villa—a tart's comeuppance.

But another memory intruded over the top of those. Another place that she had tried never to think about for a long time now. A quiet, tree-lined road, set with large, Victorian houses in spacious gardens, with fields beyond, and a river winding through the fields, through the town. Solid and prosperous, familiar and well-beloved.

Pain pierced her. And yet more guilt.

Is that why I was so eager to be swept away? Not just because of the glamour and romance, as I fooled myself into thinking, but because it blotted from my mind all the sense of loss and grief?

Her face hardened again. Well, what if it was? That was still no excuse. Even trying to make it one just cheapened her more. But self-recrimination was pointless. She was back in London, and life had to go on. She had to accept what had happened, accept her culpability—then move on. A day at a time. This dreary round would not last for ever. By the end of the summer surely she would be done with it?

The end came sooner than she had possibly dared to imagine. On the point of letting herself out of the front door on her way to work one day, she saw an envelope in her mail locker. When she saw the postmark she gazed in trepidation, then slowly opened it, dreading to read the contents. Why now, when she was not expecting such a letter? Surely it could only be bad news?

She unfolded the headed paper.

My dear Carrie, I am absolutely delighted to tell you that I have received most unexpected, and extremely welcome news...

The words danced in front of her eyes as she devoured the rest of the contents. Then she went straight back upstairs, phoned the agency to say she was quitting, cleared out her bedsit, and headed to the railway station.

She was going home.

Alexeis was in Switzerland, hunting down his mother. He didn't want to, but he knew he had no choice. It had to be done. He had to confront her for what she had done.

He could still feel the cold drenching down his spine—the sheer, blind fury misting his eyes as he heard Carrie's denunciation.

How could his mother have done that? How could she have been so monstrous as to try and pay Carrie to have an abortion? *Christos*, he knew she was obsessed—neurotically so—but surely she couldn't, just couldn't, have actively sought to end Carrie's pregnancy?

His hands clenched around the steering wheel of the car and he gunned the engine, snaking up the winding Alpine roads with greater speed. Driving the powerful car helped to absorb some of his tension, his adrenaline. Gave his mind something to focus on other than what its mission was. A mission he didn't want to carry out, but which he knew he must. His mother could not be allowed to get away with what she had done—not without his vehement condemnation.

His hands clenched harder. Between the two of them, his mother and his brother, Carrie had been chewed up and spat out. What bitter irony there was in that realisation—two people who loathed each other, and yet they had hammered Carrie from both sides, pouring their bile on her.

But it was you who made it possible. You who delivered Carrie to them—gave them the weapons to attack her with. If you hadn't used her, exploited her the way you did that evening, Yannis would not have had grounds for what he so foully called her!

And it had been the same with his mother. Cold chilled his marrow. If he hadn't made it so glaringly obvious that he had to do the decent thing and marry a woman he'd given his mother every reason to think he did not want to marry, she would not have thought to try and protect him from such a fate…

I brought it on myself. It was my fault—I gave them both the ammunition they needed.

Guilt and anger writhed like snakes within him.

They were writhing still when he arrived at the luxury clinic set high on the mountainside, nestled into pine trees, with a glorious view of the valley beneath. He gave his name at Reception, and was conducted to his mother's suite with all the deference his wealth ensured.

She was sitting out on the balcony, reading, but when he came out she lowered the book immediately, her eyes going to his face, her expression searching, tension in her features.

Alexeis gave her no time—no time to say anything.

'Carrie lost the baby.'

His mother's expression changed. He could not tell what she thought, and cared less.

'I am sorry,' she said. 'Deeply sorry.'

Emotion speared in Alexeis. His mother would be happy now—happy to think she'd saved herself five million euros! Happier still to think her precious son had been saved from the hideous fate of having to marry a woman he'd got pregnant and who would make him the worst wife possible.

'So now you can rejoice,' he said. His tone was harsh and cruel.

His eyes lasered into hers, and her face paled.

'*Rejoice?*' She said the word as if it had no meaning.

But of course it had meaning for her! It meant her precious son was safe. Blind rage misted in his eyes. He rounded on her, his voice vicious.

'Yes, *rejoice*! Of course you can! You've got exactly what you wanted—exactly what you'd have been prepared to pay five million euros for!'

Shock etched her face, but he would not let her speak.

'How could you do it?' he stormed at her. 'How could you? Something so monstrous! To want to kill my child—your own grandchild! Just because the mother was someone you didn't approve of! Didn't want for me! Because she wasn't rich! Wasn't well-connected! Wasn't *suitable* to be my wife! So you tried to bribe her with a fortune to kill her baby—tried to threaten her not to dare to marry me! You always say how much you love me, but do you call that love? *Do you?*'

'Stop! Stop—' Berenice Nicolaides's voice was harsh, but the harshness was not of anger, but of imprecation. 'Alexeis— listen to me. *Listen* to me! Listen to what I have to say!'

His eyes flashed furiously. 'What can you *possibly* say to me about what you did? That you did it for me? You did it for my sake?'

His mother's face tightened. There was anger in it now.

'Yes.' Her voice was like steel. 'I did it for you, Alexeis. For you.'

His face contorted. 'To protect me?'

'Yes. To protect you.' She leant forward slightly. 'Listen to me, Alexeis—listen to me.' Her eyes bored into his. 'I am your mother, and I will do everything in heaven and earth to safeguard your happiness. You were facing the ruination of your life!'

'So you tried to save me from it?'

She shut her eyes a moment, taking a heavy breath. Then opened them again.

'I had to find out for myself what she was, this unknown woman who was set to be your wife. I had to know, Alexeis— know what she was.' Another heavy breath escaped her. 'That is why I went to her. That is why I said to her what I said.' Her dark eyes rested remorselessly on Alexeis. 'That is why I made that obscene offer to her—offering to pay her a fortune to kill her own child. I had to know, Alexeis—I had to know if she would take it.'

There was silence—absolute silence—then Berenice Nicolaides went on, her voice low. 'You are a rich prize,

Alexeis. A prize worth getting pregnant for. But an uncertain pregnancy, threatened by miscarriage, would make a woman whose only interest was in your money more willing to consider…other offers. I had to find out if she were such a woman. So I made that devil's offer to her—coldly, deliberately, calculatingly. To find out what she was.'

Another breath scissored in her throat. 'Had she accepted my offer, I would have moved heaven and earth to enable you to take the child from her when it was born—to get complete custody of it. For its mother would have damned herself by her acceptance. But she did not accept—and in her rejection of that monstrous offer I knew… I knew she was not what I'd feared she was.'

She let the silence pool, and then she spoke again, her voice even lower. 'And I also knew I would pity her from the bottom of my heart.'

'I don't understand,' said Alexeis slowly. His mind was reeling. Everything had just turned upside down—all his assumptions, all his anger, all just…gone.

Her eyes were searching.

'Alexeis, why do you think I want you to marry an heiress? Do you think it is to make you richer still? So you can do battle with your father? Yes, that might be so, but it is not the reason that I want you to marry a rich woman. It is for *her* sake, not yours, that I want your bride to be wealthy,'

She paused, still keeping her eyes completely on him.

'Her own money will give her power,' she said. 'Power to treat you on equal terms. For the same reason I want her to be your equal in all other respects too—I want her to be beautiful, well-connected, and to move in our world. I want her mind to match yours, for her to have a career of her own, mental resources equal to yours. I want her never for one single moment to be less than your equal in any respect, by any measure. I wanted her never, for one single moment, to be at risk of being in the same position as any of your father's wives—myself included. We were all unequal to him in his eyes, and so he could despise us, exploit us—and dispose of us when he tired of us.'

Anger, rejection leapt in Alexeis's eyes. 'I am not my father!'

'You enjoy many of his advantages,' she riposted. 'Advantages which you could choose to abuse and exploit, as he does. Like him, you are rich and handsome, and you have a formidable business intelligence. You take what you want from life—especially women, Alexeis. You choose the ones you want, and when you have done with them you dispose of them. Oh, you only choose those who can cope with that treatment—perhaps even deserve no better. For the reason they let themselves be chosen by you is all the worldly advantages you bring. And perhaps your attitude towards them doesn't matter when your women are like that—but what if a woman is not, Alexeis? What then?'

She took a breath. 'That was why, when she rejected my offer of an abortion, I knew I could only pity her for having to marry you. It is not a fate I would wish on any such girl. You would not be cruel to her, as your father was, but she would have been unhappy all the same. Unhappy all her life with you, knowing she was chaining a man who did not want to be married to her. Knowing that all she had to offer was her beauty, the appeal of your sexual desire for her—a desire that would fade as she aged, a desire that you would tire of.'

For a moment there was complete silence. Then Alexeis spoke.

'You're wrong.'

It was all he said, but it made something change, minutely, in his mother's face. His eyes rested on her.

'You're wrong,' he said again. 'Completely, totally, absolutely wrong.'

'Am I?' said his mother. Her voice was low, but what was in her eyes was an intensity of focus.

'Yes,' said her son. 'More wrong than you have ever been—more wrong than it is possible to be.'

'And what,' she said, with the same intensity of focus in her gaze, 'are you going to do about this wrongness of mine?'

He reached forward and took her hand. Her fingers clutched his, and he pressed them in return.

'What I must do,' he said.

'Must you?' she said. Her voice was strange, strained. 'Fate has taken the responsibility for her from you—freed you from so unsuitable a wife, who would be so unhappy with you. You no longer need to be honourable.'

'You're wrong,' he answered. 'I must do this. Without question or hesitation or doubt I must do it—or my life—' his eyes rested on his mother's face '—my life has no meaning any more.'

For one long, last moment she gazed up at him. And then into her eyes tears pooled. Her fingers pressed on his one long, last moment, and then she slipped her hand from his.

'Go, then,' she said. 'Go after her. And when you find her…' her tears were like diamonds '…give her my blessing and my undying gratitude.'

Their eyes met and held.

'God speed,' she said softly.

He bent to kiss her cheek, and was gone.

The powerful car ate up the miles, snaking back down the mountainside. Alexeis drove fast, and purposefully. The world around him in the crystal Alpine air was in super-focus. His whole life was in super-focus. He could see everything with a searing clarity, as if through a lens that sharpened every sense.

He knew exactly what he was doing.

The way was clear now.

Wonder seized him, and disbelief. How had he not seen? How had he not known? How had he blinded himself for so long?

How could it be that it had taken his brother, with all the sensitivity of a block of wood when it came to relations with women, to bring him up short like that? How could it be that it had taken his mother—his mother who had been obsessed, he'd always thought, with him marrying an heiress as part of her vendetta against his father—to make him face the truth? A truth he had just never dreamt of—never once considered.

A truth he knew, with pain and shame, that had had to be forged in the crucible of Carrie's pregnancy and tragic miscarriage, her hurt and angry rejection of him.

A chill went through him.

I might never have realised what was happening to me. Just continued on my hedonistic, pleasurable path—enjoying Carrie, nothing more. Never facing up to what was starting to happen. Never even realising.

There had been glimpses, signs and portents, that, had he had the slightest kind of self-awareness, he might have recognised. Might have pointed him the way.

I stopped on impulse as she walked along. Picked her up off the street. Something I'd never done before—never. So why—why did I do it for her? What made me do it? What made me so sure that something so...outrageous...was so right? A woman I'd seen only for a handful of moments.

But something, something about her called to me.

And there had been more.

He'd taken her with him on his business travels. That was something he'd never done. Yes, she hadn't got any kind of career to tie her down, but that hadn't been the reason. He'd never *wanted* to take any of her predecessors with him. But he'd wanted Carrie with him. So what was it about her that had made him want to do so?

She had been completely different from all his previous women. Novelty value, he'd called it, but it hadn't worn off—her appeal for him was still just as strong as it ever had been that very first night. An appeal that no other woman had ever had for him—an appeal that, time after time after time, had been…special. Different.

Unforgettable. Every time.

And it wasn't just sex that he wanted her for.

That was what made her different—that it was her I wanted, not just her body. I just wanted to be with her.

Emotion flooded through him, making his hands grip the wheel.

I just wanted to be with her. She gave me something I'd never known—a peace, a quietness of the mind, a comfort of the body. She was a woman I could just sit with, be with, lie beside.

And it had been that that had overridden anything else, *everything* else.

We were good together.

It was that simple.

In the end, nothing else about her mattered. Nothing. He just wanted to be with her.

For the rest of his life.

If she would have him.

CHAPTER TWELVE

CARRIE walked along through the park, heading for the far side. It was wonderful to be home, she told herself. Wonderful to be back in the town she'd grown up in, that she'd lived in all her life. Everything was as familiar to her as if she had only yesterday boarded the train, heartsore and grieving, to head for London.

It was as if she had never left.

But that wasn't true, of course. Things had happened to her that had changed her for ever.

Alexeis Nicolaides had happened to her.

And she had conceived and lost his child.

Despite all her strenuous efforts, all her relief and gladness to be back home again, to be welcomed by those she had known all her life, and to have a future to look forward to, she could still feel haunting her the knowledge and the memory and worst of all the dreams that pressed like ghosts against a windowpane.

Would she one day be free of them? Surely she must? Surely one day the dreams would stop, the memories would dim, and he would disappear, would cease to be? Just as the brief, fragile life within her had ceased. Yet it seemed almost as if with each passing day—even though she had so much now to shut out the memories, to divert and occupy her mind and attention—that when they did break through they were more powerful, more vivid than before.

Sometimes, just for a glimpse, she could almost feel she was seeing him—seeing the tall, familiar figure glancing at her, those dark, long-lashed eyes washing over her, making her weak and breathless and boneless, filling her with aching, longing…

And then with bleak, black loathing…

That was what she had to cling to. Not the quickening heart-rate, the catch of her breath, the aching inside her. No—the bleak, black loathing. That was all she must feel.

But better to feel nothing at all. Better by far to immerse herself in the new reality of her life—even pierced as it was by the sorrow of her father's death, with memories of him vivid in every street, every place she was.

The old house was gone—long sold— and though it was a loss, she knew it was for the best, in that it would only have been even sadder to be there without her father. Better to accept the lodgings she had found—simple, but comfortable, and affordable and close to where she needed to be.

And though, yes, it was true there was a stabbing poignancy about being in Marchester without her father, and sometimes it was hard, *very* hard, to accept that he was gone, she must take comfort in knowing that she was doing what he had wanted her to do. And it was just what she had longed for, so she must appreciate it, value it, sink herself into it. Above all, she must face the future, walk forward into it clear-eyed, without looking back to something that had been just a mirage, an illusion. A self-deceiving delusion, spiralling down and down into humiliation and shame. A lesson she had bitterly, bitterly learnt. And now she must move forward, however much the past sought to suck her back into its tempting, deceitful power.

Going forward was the only way. The future ahead the only possibility. A good future, a satisfying future, a challenging future and an ordained future—the one she had always assumed would be her life, her work. And now it had begun, earlier than she had dreamt possible, taking her as far as she could possibly be from that glittering, seductive mirage that had beguiled and lured her.

She quickened her pace, glancing at the clock on the tower ahead of her, across the wide paved area on the far side of the park. Her feet were shod with canvas shoes, a million miles away from the delicate fine leather sandals she'd once worn. The simple cotton dress too was a million miles from the designer clothes that had until so recently adorned her. The bag over her shoulder was large, and stuffed full with everything she needed. Her hair was fastened neatly at the back of her neck and plaited tightly, as if it had never poured richly, in tousled, wanton tresses, over bare sun-kissed shoulders. Well, now she *needed* sensible clothes and shoes, a capacious bag, hair that was kept out of the way, a face that needed no more maintenance than soap and water and swift moisturiser. Anything else would have been superfluous.

What did she care about her looks now? She had never cared much about them, never considered them—for those around her had not been interested in them. And in London they had brought her either harassment or embarrassment, or both.

And the attentions of a man who—

No! She was doing it again—thinking about him, remembering him, conjuring him into her mind. Letting in that dark, deceptive glamour that had swept her away and made such a humiliating fool of her—and for which so high a price had been paid.

She passed through the Victorian wrought-iron gateway

from the park and paused on the pavement, waiting for a break in the traffic. Her eyes went to the wide flight of steps leading up to the imposing building across the busy concourse. A familiar sight, and one that had so very often included the figure of her father, walking down, his brow creased in concentration, his mind far from the outside world. Grief plucked at her. She knew that never again would she see that sight outside of her memory.

Did I do the right thing, coming back home? I know it is what he would have wanted—what I have always wanted—and everyone has been so kind to me. And yet… And yet it's harder than I realized—to be here, to pick up the reins of my life again.

Even as the thoughts moved in her mind, others came in their wake, bringing images, vivid and intrusive. New experiences—wonderful, exciting, filled with glamour and passion. And desire—*no*! Urgently she crushed down her wayward thoughts. No. Alexeis Nicolaides had made sex unforgettable because he happened to be very good at it—he had, after all, she reminded herself with deliberate cynicism, enough experience to be very good! But being good in bed was not enough. Nowhere near enough. However mesmerising he was, she must never, never forget what he had stooped to. Never forget what his assumptions about her had been.

Never forget how he held you so close, how he kissed you. With passion, but more than passion, with tenderness and sensitivity and delight. Never forget how you lay in his arms, safe, protected, contented. At peace. And happy…so very, very happy.

But forgetting was exactly what she *must* do! Of course she must!

Even if the ending had not been so terrible you would have had to forget it, forget him—for eventually he would have tired of you, sent you away. It would have been over…

Her eyes clouded. Well, it was over, all right. Over more absolutely, more terminally, than any affair could ever be. It had imploded, hideously, with her realisation of the truth—and the sad agony of her miscarriage had underwritten the end in tragic culmination.

Unconsciously her hand went to her abdomen, hovering, before dropping away. Her face shadowed. Words formed in her mind. The most dangerous words in the world.

What if…?

No—again and again, *no*. She must not let her mind go down that dangerous path. Every reason, every logic told her that. That door was sealed closed. For ever.

She knew, *knew* the right answer—knew that she must never knock upon that door.

A gap in the traffic came, and she headed out across the roadway—brisk, purposeful, striding towards the future. The only future she had. The only future she wanted.

Alexeis eased the throttle and let the car accelerate along the motorway. His nerves were stretched to breaking point. They had been for day after day. How long ago it seemed since he had driven down the mountain in Switzerland, his whole being fused into one point—to find again what he had lost. To win back what he had driven away.

To win back Carrie.

It was his sole purpose. His only goal.

It was very simple, very straightforward.

Except for one thing. One thing he had completely not envisaged. He hadn't been able to find her. *How had she disappeared? How could she just disappear?*

He had never for a moment considered it. At Zurich airport he'd phoned his London office, instructing his PA to find the address of Carrie's bedsit. He'd had no idea where it was, apart from her mentioning that it was in Paddington.

However, one of his drivers had taken her that first afternoon from the Knightsbridge store, had stopped at her bedsit to give her time to get her passport and any other personal items before driving on to Heathrow to rendezvous with him. So all that was necessary was to quiz the driver and find out where he'd taken Carrie that afternoon.

But when Alexeis had landed in London, his PA had phoned to say the driver in question was on holiday and out of contact. Irritated, Alexeis had told his PA to track down the employment agency who had found her work at the gallery. But they had said Carrie was no longer on their books, and that they could give out no personal details of any kind. Eventually, after a tiresome and difficult search, he had found Carrie's bedsit—only to discover from one of Carrie's neighbours that she had given it up and moved out.

He'd gone right back to square one, and two frustrating weeks had been wasted. Worse, he'd then had to suspend his search for her when he'd had to return to Greece—unwillingly—to take a board meeting that his father had not bothered to attend. Never had work so irritated him or seemed such a waste of his precious time. He didn't want to do it—couldn't care less about it. Wanted only to be shot of it. He seemed to have tunnel vision on only the one thing he really wanted.

To find Carrie.

Where the hell was she?

The question had burned in him, frustrating and nerve-racking.

His team of investigators were worse than useless, it seemed. There were, so they had informed him, a very large number of people with her surname, and with no indication of even what part of the country she might be in, the search would inevitably be long. Frustratingly, he had realized he did not even know her date of birth.

Did she have other forenames? Alexeis had been asked, politely but pressingly. None that he knew of. Did he know where she came from? Where she was brought up? Where she went to school? Anything like that? Did he know people who knew her—friends, relatives, former employers—anyone at all? No, no and no. She'd worked in London—temporary jobs, temporary accommodation—that was all he knew.

When it had come to finding the one person in the whole world he *had* to find, the truth had been grim. Carrie could be anywhere—anywhere at all. She might—and the thought had struck a chill in him—not even be in the country…

He'd had absolutely no lead on her whatsoever. Nothing.

And then, like a bolt from the blue, a strand of memory had been activated in his mind—plucked from who knew where. The fragments of something he'd asked Carrie in passing that very first evening, when his only purpose in conversation had been to set her at ease. He'd been paying almost no attention to what she'd said—his mind had been on other things.

But out of some dusty corner something had percolated up. He'd asked her something about liking living in London, and her answer had been surprisingly negative for a girl so beautiful. And then hadn't he asked her where she came from? He had—he was sure of it. But what had she said?

Her voice floated distantly… 'It's a small town, sort of in the Midlands.'

Yes, but *which* town? Frustration bit. He'd racked his brain. Had she said it by name? If so, *what* name? What letter had it started with?

M—that was the first letter!

A sense of triumph had gripped him. OK, he had something now. The moment his plane had landed, he'd been on the phone to London. Then he'd rerouted there himself.

Marchester. That had been the name she'd said. None of the other possibilities his investigators had suggested rang the same bell.

What if she'd gone back there? She'd said she hated London, so why not go home?

He had dredged his memory again. Hadn't she said something about her father dying a while back? But maybe there was other family there? Or friends she had gone to? And even if she hadn't gone back there, they might know where she was.

For the first time in weeks, his mood had cheered notably. Even when he'd been informed of the depressingly large number of people in the city listed in the electoral rolls and telephone directories with the surname Richards he had still not been disheartened. Leaving his team to methodically work their way through, until they found either her or someone who knew her, he had set off up the motorway without delay.

He could wait not a moment longer. The imperative to find her was absolute. Overwhelming. It consumed his whole being.

Because without Carrie his life would have no meaning.

And whatever life she wanted with him, she would have. If she hated crowds, felt uneasy or insecure in company, then they wouldn't have any. If she didn't want to go to parties where the talk was of art and literature, then they wouldn't. If she didn't enjoy opera he'd never go to another one all his life. If she didn't like travelling, they wouldn't. It was very simple. He would live anywhere in the world she wanted to live, in any way that she wanted. Do anything she wanted.

He had money to burn—and no responsibilities but Carrie. He could forfeit running the Nicolaides Group—make his father take on the task again, or simply appoint an external CEO. It didn't matter. Nothing mattered. Only Carrie.

And—his heart seemed to squeeze as he voiced the thought—if Carrie wanted a dozen children right now, oh, dear God, he would be honoured beyond all things to raise them with her…

The vice squeezed tighter. And if anyone, anyone at all, ever tried to put her down, to make her feel inferior, insecure in any way, any way at all, if they showed the slightest sign of disrespect or disapproval—well, they would be sorry, that was all.

Because Carrie was far, far more precious than anything else in his life.

The most precious thing in the world to him.

And he had to find her—he *had* to!

Urgency, desperation filled him. His foot pressed down on the accelerator.

By the time he arrived at Marchester, he had already received from his investigators five addresses for people called Richards. None was Carrie, but they might be relatives. His investigators were currently making phone contact, and would keep him updated. As he eased the car forward into traffic, heading for the city centre, Alexeis wondered why he hadn't just had the patience to wait until an actual address had been found for Carrie. She might not even be living here any more, he reminded himself. But patience was not his forte—and there was a gut feeling in him that told him she had come back to her home town. She was here somewhere. He knew it.

She had to be—she just had to be!

But he also acknowledged she was most likely to be working at the moment. It was only mid-morning. So far his team had drawn a blank with the local job agencies—none had a Carrie Richards on their books. Well, maybe she hadn't got a job through an agency. Maybe she knew local employers well enough to approach them directly. He had instructed his investigators to check out restaurants and catering companies. They were also checking out colleges of further education. He hadn't forgotten suggesting to her that she had a natural talent for massage, and for all he knew, she'd gone and signed up for some kind of training and qualification. She *must* be capable of something more than waitressing. Massage, beautician, therapist—those sorts of jobs would be ideal for her.

He glanced around, as if he might spot just that kind of establishment. The kind of college that taught such courses would not be in the city centre, however. Apart from its grandiose Victorian civic edifices, including an imposing nineteenth century town hall, the city centre was dominated by the buildings associated with the University of Marchester, which was, so he had recently learnt, during his determined enquiries, one of the premier redbrick universities in the UK. It wouldn't be the sort of place to run the kind of course that Carrie would be likely to follow.

He was approaching the university area now. To his left, a large Victorian city park, with iron railings marching along the pavement, and to his right a white-stuccoed building with a flight of steps and surmounted by a clock tower. Right in front of him was a pedestrian crossing, with the lights changing to red. He decelerated, waiting behind several other cars, the powerful note of the engine throbbing. A couple of males walking along the pavement turned their heads automatically, taking in the powerful, high-performance car that habitually graced the covers of aspirational car magazines. Alexeis paid them no attention, merely keeping the engine idling and drumming his fingers on the steering wheel, his eyes peeled on the lights, ready for them to change.

Until, for no reason he could discern, he glanced to the pedestrians crossing.

One of them was Carrie.

Carrie's eyes were focussed on the pavement, and then the wide paved area beyond, leading up to the broad white flight of steps, flanked on either side by parking bays. But as she gained it and started across the concourse, hefting her heavy bag slightly, she suddenly heard the roar of an engine, and then a dark blue car was shooting past her, right into an empty parking bay clearly marked 'Head of Geological Sciences'. Carrie stared. Surely that low, lean, growling monster was not the kind of car to be driven by a crusty professor of geology.

A moment later all such thoughts—all thoughts completely—were gone.

Alexeis Nicolaides was striding towards her.

She froze. What else could she do? Every muscle and tendon in her body had just stopped.

It was Alexeis—

He was all she could see. All she could do was just stare blankly at him as he strode towards her, purposeful, heading right for her.

Alexeis.

Emotion leapt in her—she didn't know what it was, or why, only that it was overpowering. Adrenaline surged.

Flight! That was what it wanted! That was why it had surged in her! She turned, almost running, blindly, instinctively. The university bookshop was ahead of her, and if she could get in there she might escape him, evade him. She plunged inside, blinking in the sudden gloom, then heading further in.

Her arm was seized. She was spun round.

'Carrie!'

Her eyes flared. He was standing over her—so tall, so overpowering. 'I came to find you! I've been searching everywhere for you! I have to talk to you—I have to!'

She was helpless, numbed and stricken, disbelieving and in shock. Feebly, she let him guide her to the deserted rear of the bookshop, sit her down at a narrow reading table enclosed by toweringly high bookshelves. Her heavy bag clunked on the surface of the table He lowered his tall frame into the chair opposite it.

She stared at him, her eyes wide with shock.

Alexeis—it was Alexeis. Here, now, in Marchester.

But why? Why? Why was he here? Why was he looking for her?

She stared, trying to make her brain work. But it didn't seem to want to work at all. It was as if it was suffering from some kind of overload of emotion. She didn't know what the emotion was, just that it was sweeping through her head like a hurricane.

'I have to talk to you.'

His voice was low, urgent. Insistent.

Somehow, though her mouth was suddenly as dry as a bone, Carrie forced herself to speak.

'There is nothing to say. It was all said.'

Her voice grated out through a throat that had closed completely.

His hand slashed negation.

'No. It wasn't. It wasn't all said at all! That's the reason I've been searching for you. It *wasn't* all said, Carrie. The most important bit got left out. I was so devastated with what you threw at me, I let you go. I let you leave me. I should never have done that—never! I should have told you then! But I didn't realise—didn't realise that—'

He broke off.

'I want you back,' he said simply.

Because that was what it was. Simple. Unarguable. Irrefutable.

Her expression changed. 'You must be mad to think that.'

'No. Saner than I've ever been.'

Something moved in her eyes. 'I mean mad to think I would come back. Come back to be your bimbo, your tart.' She spoke in a low voice, intense and bitter.

'No!' The hand slashed through the air again. 'You were never that—you were never that! You don't believe me, but it is true, Carrie, I swear it. What I did to you on Lefkali, that evening at my mother's villa, was unforgivable. I know that, and I beg your forgiveness. I used you abominably and I am deeply, deeply ashamed of having done so. You were never—not for an instant—what I painted you as for my own malign, selfish purposes! But I beg you, do not judge me only for the way I was on Lefkali with you! When we were together in America, in Italy—when you were there with me—you were—you were—'

He closed his eyes as a million memories seared at once. His eyes opened again, seeing her in front of him once more. He would never let her leave him again.

'Special,' he said. His voice had dropped. 'You were special to me, Carrie. More special that I could realise—until you left me. More special to me than any woman has ever been—than any woman will ever be.'

He took a breath, his eyes holding hers. She was sitting so still, not moving at all.

'I want you to marry me,' he said.

For a long, long moment, she simply looked at him. Then, in a low, tight voice, she spoke.

'I've had an offer of marriage from you before. When you

told me you were prepared to marry me. Forcing yourself to marry me simply because I'd got myself pregnant with your baby. Steeling yourself to take me as your wife because you had no alternative but to do so. Resenting utterly the fact you had to do so. And then—' her eyes bored into his without mercy '—you were blessed by the fate that removed the grim necessity from you. No baby, so no marriage—reprieved in the nick of time!'

His face had blanched.

'Carrie—no. If you believe nothing else of what I say, believe this. I never, not for a moment, wanted you to lose the baby. Never. Acquit me of nothing else, if you will, but that. I am sorry beyond all things that you had to go through that ordeal—and to know that you would have preferred to give our child away to strangers than to raise it with me fills me with a guilt I can't assuage. But I also know—' a harsh breath was torn from him '—I also know that it took that day, that last, terrible day, when you threw everything at me, it took the terrible emptiness inside of me knowing you were gone, knowing I had neither child nor you for all my life, for all the rest of my days ahead, to open my eyes, to make me realise—'

He stopped short. Then slowly, heavily, continued.

'To make me realise just what you are to me. The most important person in the world to me.' His eyes held hers. 'I want you with me. Now and for ever.' He took another breath. 'And if you hate my lifestyle, I'll change it. I'll stop running the company—my father can do the work. I want only to be with you—wherever you want to be, living however you want to live. When I thought we would marry because of the baby, I worried that you would hate being Mrs Alexeis Nicolaides, having to be a society hostess, but we don't have to do that! We can live like recluses, just you and me, sailing away into the sunset.'

She was looking at him strangely. 'Hiding away the bimbo? Tucking her out of sight?'

'No!' he said vehemently. 'Carrie, that's not, *not* what I meant! I want to make you happy—that's all! I don't want you ever feeling looked down on, or subjected to the kind of disparagement that you felt when you were with me.'

There was still the same strange look in her eyes. 'You mean on account of my being stupid?' Her voice was flat.

Anger flared in his eyes. 'There have been people in this world whose staggering intelligence has brought only misery and destruction in its wake. That isn't virtue. *You* have virtue, Carrie. You have everything—everything that is important. You have kindness and sweetness. The man fortunate enough to be your husband would be privileged beyond imagination.'

'Do you mean that?' she asked in a low voice.

'Yes—without doubt, without hesitation. Adamantly and absolutely. It is that that is important. Nothing else.'

Her eyes slid away, dropping. 'But is it? Is it all that is important?' Her eyes went back to him, and their expression was troubled. 'I'm so very different, Alexeis—from the women you know, the life you lead. You say you could give it up, but you would get bored. What would we talk about?'

'What did we ever talk about? Did you see me bored in your company?' He caught her hand. 'Carrie, what we had was so special—I got a glimpse of it, but I didn't realise just how special it was. Only that it—that it brought me a peace I had never known. A peace I only had with you. There was a rightness about being with you. It's all I want, Carrie.' He paused, as if steeling himself, then said it. 'Just because you never got much of an education—that was *not* your fault! How could anyone blame you for it—judge you on it? And as my wife who would care what education you got? You need be nothing *but* my wife—'

'Your bimbo wife?'

He swore. It was in Greek, which was just as well.

'If you say that word about yourself one more time—'

'Stupid, then. Dim. Not too bright. Only one brain cell. Sweet, but thick. That's what you think of me, isn't it? Isn't it? It doesn't matter if you're trying to be nice about it—or kind, or sensitive, or whatever—in the end you don't think I'm your intellectual equal. You think I'm a sweet, kind, pretty, beddable sort of woman, different from any others you've had affairs with, and because of that you fancy you should marry me—despite all the differences between us!'

For a moment, a long moment, he was silent. Her heart was thumping in her chest.

'No.' His voice was low. 'I want you to marry me for one very clear reason. I have fallen in love with you.'

Between them, the silence stretched.

'And if you love someone, Carrie, you don't care about anything else. When you love someone, the differences disappear. They just—cease to exist. After all—' his eyes held hers, on an unbreakable chain '—isn't it the same for you?'

She paled.

She could not answer—could not.

Must not.

Everything she knew about what she had been to Alexeis she summoned to her mind. Urgently. Desperately. The litany that had marched through her mind day after day—every accusation against him, every accusation against herself, every reason for hatred and guilt—she sought to marshal yet again. Because she had to. It was entirely necessary to do so. Essential.

Because what else could defend her against what he had just said? What else was strong enough to defeat that?

But he had taken all her accusations and countered them.

Confessed to them or repudiated them. They were useless now—useless. Every one of them. Broken in her hands.

She could only stare at him—stare at him with anguished eyes.

'Tell me, Carrie. Tell me if that is not true!' His voice was low and urgent. 'Tell me!'

'I told myself I wasn't like that poor, silly Madame Butterfly.' Her words were halting, strained. 'Not just because I never had to bear the child of a man to whom I was nothing more than an amusement, a novelty.' His face blanched, but she went on, remorseless, impelling. 'But because of one vital, overwhelming difference. I didn't fall in love with you. Stupid I may have been—but not that stupid. I clung to that— clung to it desperately when I had to face the truth about you. But you've knocked down those truths I hated you for— knocked them all down except one. That last one.'

Her eyes searched his.

'Do you believe it, Alexeis? Do you truly believe that love makes all differences disappear, cease to exist?'

There was an intensity in her voice that stretched it like tautened wire.

He did not hesitate. Not for a moment, not for a second.

'Yes. With all my heart.'

He reached towards her hand to take it in his, desperate to hold her again, hold any part of her. But there was someone coming past the bookshelves—one of the sales assistants, heading to the storeroom. Alexeis saw her eyes go automatically to him, as women's usually did. But then her glance went past him to Carrie. The woman stopped.

'Oh,' she said brightly, 'just the person. I must have missed you coming in. Are you here to collect the books you ordered, Dr Richards?'

CHAPTER THIRTEEN

SHE wasn't sure what she said to the sales assistant, didn't register that the woman had nodded and gone through to the storeroom. Registered only that a hand like steel had gripped around her wrist.

'*What* did that woman call you?'

Carrie rested her eyes on Alexeis's face, where blank stupefaction and disbelief registered across it.

'She called me Dr Richards,' she said. Her voice was expressionless. 'Because that's who I am. I got my PhD last year—the year my father died. He was a senior research fellow here at the university, and I've just taken up a postdoctoral research post in his former department.'

His eyes were on her, quite blank. Then his gaze moved down to her bag, lying on the table, its contents starting to spill. His hand released her. Went instead to the first book resting on the top.

'"Tyrosine Kinase Inhibitors and Human Neoplasia,"' he read out.

'Biochemistry,' said Carrie, in that same inexpressive voice. 'My research area is oncogene expression. That's how genes involved in tumour development come to be switched on, causing cancer, and how they can be switched off to cure it. It was my father's area of research as well—he continued working up to the very end.'

She looked away. It was still so painful to think of just how driven her father had been—determined to live as long as he could, to keep his research going.

'The more we discover, the more we can cure,' he would say, ignoring the pain racking him from the very tumours he was seeking to understand and vanquish.

'Why the charade as a waitress?' The harshness in Alexeis's voice banished her father's ghost.

'It wasn't a charade,' she answered levelly. 'My father managed to live eighteen months beyond his prognosis, by taking life-extending drugs that are not available on the health service. They were extremely expensive, and to pay for them our house was remortgaged—with the result that when he died what didn't go in taxes went to repay the mortgage. It was something I agreed to willingly—not just because it gave me precious extra time with him, but because his work was everything to him, and his frustration at being taken from it was overwhelming. He left me all his research data and, although I had to leave Marchester, one of the colleagues he'd worked closely with, based at London University, worked with me to write it up for publication. I spent my days doing that, but I had to earn my keep as well, so I took on casual labour in the evening. When…when I met you, I'd just finally sent off my father's typescript. But I'd decided to go on working in London, doing what I could, knowing I had been accepted for the post-doctoral research post here, in the new academic year.'

She took a breath. 'Shortly after I came back to London from Lefkali, I had very unexpected news. My supervisor wrote to me, saying that some extra funding had been found and I could take up my post straight away. So I came back here.'

He was silent a moment.

'Did you enjoy making a fool of me, Carrie? Pretending you weren't what you are?' The harshness was unabated.

Her expression tensed. 'I didn't make a fool of you, Alexeis. I've spent all my life in scientific academia. My mother was a physiologist, my father a biochemist. It's all I ever really knew. About everything else I'm very ignorant. I know very little history, nothing about art or literature or opera, or economics or politics. I don't have any scintillating conversation about things. I just know biochemistry. But if you start talking biochemistry to most people their eyes glaze over. I learnt not to say much, not having anything much to say about things that weren't to do with biochemistry. And I also learnt—'

She stopped abruptly.

'Go on,' he said.

Her eyes flashed momentarily. 'I learnt that men who go for pretty blondes don't like it when they find out she's got a PhD!'

'So you act dumb?' he said coldly.

'What do you think I should do?' she riposted. 'Announce to people that I'm a post-doctoral biochemist? Slip it subtly into conversation? "Oh, and what do you do? I'm in investment banking myself." That sort of thing? No, thank you!'

His mouth tightened. 'You could have told me, all the same.'

She gave a half-shrug. 'What for? It didn't seem very relevant at the time.' Her voice thinned. 'But then you see, Alexeis, I never actually realised you thought me a bimbo. I didn't know I had to prove to you I wasn't.'

A line of colour stained his cheekbones, but he retaliated. 'Did you think it would put me off you?'

She hesitated a fatal fraction of a second. 'I was living in what I thought was a fantasy,' she said in a low voice. 'Not the world that was real to me. The world I live in—this world.' She nodded around the bookshop, lined with shelves and shelves of academic tomes. 'It's pretty short on drop-dead millionaires who sweep you off your feet and dress you up like a princess and waft you around the world in private jets!' Her mouth pressed thinly. 'I meant what I said to you on Lefkali, Alexeis. I blinded myself deliberately to what I was doing with you. And what does it matter—' self-accusation edged her voice '—whether I did that as a bimbo waitress or a pretty blonde PhD?'

'Nothing,' he said. 'It matters nothing. Because what we had wasn't tacky or sordid. It was never that. Tell me something—tell me truthfully.'

Dark, lambent eyes rested on her, not letting her go. She felt their power, felt her weakness. Oh, dear God, such weakness...

'Tell me,' said Alexeis, 'if I had taken you to...to Benidorm, because it was all I could afford, and expected you to pay half, would you have come with me, Carrie? *Would* you?'

She felt her chest tighten. The power of his eyes was still holding her.

'Yes,' she whispered, because it was all she could do.

'And if I were just a waiter, would you have come with me—*would* you?'

'Yes...' The whisper was fainter.

'And if I reach across the table now—' his hand moved, stretching out to curve around her wrist, not tightly now, not like steel, but like a silken noose '—and draw you to me—' his other hand reached to slide around her nape, the gentle pressure of his fingertips sending a million nerve-endings tingling into life, making her breath catch, her eyes widen hopelessly, helplessly, as his mouth brushed against hers, cool and tender, dissolving her body and her soul into his own '—will you come with me now, for the rest of your life? Will you, Dr Carrie Richards, whom I love,' he breathed, 'so much?'

She shut her eyes. It was all she could do as his mouth moved on hers sweetly—possessively.

Emotion poured through her. An unstoppable tide.

There was a sound of a throat clearing, and an embarrassed little cough.

Guiltily, Carrie pulled free of Alexeis.

Two learned tomes were placed in front of her. 'Your books, Dr Richards,' said the sales assistant.

'Oh—thank you,' she said, cheeks firing red.

'I'll put them on your account, shall I?' said the assistant.

'Um, yes—thank you.'

'Although,' said the woman, and Carrie could see her eyes going, as every female eye in the universe would surely go, to the man sitting opposite her, 'you may just find you don't have the time to read them,' she finished dryly—and just a tad enviously. Then she whisked away.

Alexeis slid his fingers into hers. Meshing tight.

'You know,' he said contemplatively, 'if this university is anything like the one I went to, I suspect that the news that the most beautiful post-doc on campus is in the process of being seduced by some Greek Lothario will race round faster than the speed of light. Which, if I remember my school physics well enough, is something in the region of three hundred thousand metres a second—'

'You're showing off,' said Carrie.

Long lashes swept down over his dark eyes.

'Only to you. And I would far rather show off to you by making you the best and most devoted husband that any girl—bimbo or brainbox—could ever, ever want.' His hand tightened on hers. 'Please marry me. I love you, and I think that you love me, I pray that you love me. And if you don't quite yet, then I will strive with all my might to win your love.' He took a breath. 'I said before we would live wherever you wanted to live, and I'm sure there are wonderful, wonderful places to live around here, so that you can do your work.' He took another breath, sharper this time, with an edge of pain in it. 'And one day, when the time is right for you, I hope most humbly that we will be given a second chance to become parents.'

Carrie's eyes shadowed. 'The doctor told me that there was probably something wrong with the embryo, and that was why I miscarried. In my head I know that, but—' She broke off, tears sparking in her eyes.

He cupped her cheek. 'When the time is right, my dearest darling one, then you will make the best mother any child could have.' His own eyes shadowed. 'I knew that then, even on Lefkali. I knew that any child with you would be loved and cherished.'

He had said it to comfort her, but instead her eyes hardened.

'Your mother did not think so. She thought I'd kill my baby in exchange for her foul money!' There was a stoniness in her expression that Alexeis knew he had to allay.

'She was wrong to speak to you that way, Carrie, but she never meant it. Not for a moment. When I accused her, she told me she said it only to test you, Carrie.' His voice was sad. 'All she knew of you was that vile, distorted picture I painted of you. She was terrified you had deliberately sought to entrap me, and she thought that offering you a fortune to have an abortion would show whether you were not fit to be my wife.' He took a heavy breath. 'Carrie, if you cannot forgive her, I understand, but...' his expression changed '...she sent me after you, to find you—because I told her that without you my life had no meaning. I came to find you with her blessing, my dearest one.'

She stared at him. 'But she cannot wish me as your wife. How could she? You said she wants an heiress for you.'

A self-condemning twist formed at Alexeis's mouth. 'That was for my future wife's benefit, apparently, not mine. My mother brought no money to her marriage, only her position in society, which my father did not have, being "new" money. Once he'd married her, he acquired her status, and so after I was born, and she could have no more children, she became—superfluous. She did not want that for my wife.'

His mouth tightened, and he looked at her straightly.

'We haven't been a happy family. There has been misery and bitterness and anger and hatred. But now it ends. I won't bring that ugly heritage into our marriage.' His expression changed, lightened. 'What I *will* bring is a Nicolaides wife who will never be another Kryia Nicolaides! You, my darling—' he lifted her hand and raised it to his lips, a smile on his mouth and a speaking expression in his eyes '—will be *Dr* Nicolaides.'

He drew her to her feet and tucked her hand into his crooked arm, casually hooking her bulging bag effortlessly from a finger over his shoulder while Carrie picked up her new textbooks.

'*Dr* Nicolaides,' he said again happily, as he started to stroll with her to the door. 'The first doctor in our family! You cannot imagine, my loved one, with what smugness I shall introduce you as *Dr* Nicolaides! How stunned everyone will be to realise that I have a wife who is not only the loveliest woman on God's earth, but who is *Dr* Nicolaides as well! They will say to me, "Alexeis—how have you the infernal luck to be married to so beautiful a bride who is also a *Dr* Nicolaides?" And I will say to them—'

'You know,' said Carrie, cutting him short, 'I think I preferred it when you thought I was a bimbo. It definitely had its advantages!'

'What's that you say, *Dr* Nicolaides-to-be?' he queried exaggeratedly.

'If you call me *Dr* once more, I'll hit you with this book on heat shock proteins and their role in immunotherapy!' said Carrie roundly. 'And don't believe I wouldn't. I slapped you brother—'

Alexeis laughed. 'Good for you—he deserved it. And he certainly deserved it when I slugged him for calling you a hot little bimbo.'

Carrie stared, a warm glow starting in her. 'Did you?'

'Yes. And the thing was,' he said contemplatively, walking her out onto the pavement, 'when he said something similarly offensive about Adrianna and Marissa I didn't even twitch. Apparently…' he glanced at Carrie '…Yannis said he was giving me a lesson.'

'In what?'

Alexei's eyes glinted. 'In finally being smart enough to realise why I red-misted when anyone called you a bimbo. You included. It took me a while—I'm not as clever as you, you see—so—'

He broke off. Standing behind his car was one of the university's beadles, and behind him, in a very ancient Morris Traveller, an elderly man was gesticulating angrily through the open window.

'Uh-oh,' said Alexeis. He strode over, with Carrie hurrying to keep up.

'Professor Carlyle, I'm most terribly sorry,' she began hastily, addressing the famously short-tempered head of geology. 'It's all my fault that this car is in your parking space.'

Irate myopic eyes were turned on her with considerable force.

'Who are you?' demanded the professor of geological sciences.

'I'm Jonathan Richards's daughter, Professor.'

He stared. 'Good Lord, so you are! Well, that's all very well, but—'

'Professor.' A smooth, authoritative voice sounded behind Carrie. 'I shall remove my car instantly. Please accept my unreserved apologies.'

The beadle came forward. 'There's a fine for parking in reserved spaces,' he announced. 'We have to level them, or the students would all park there.'

'Of course,' said Alexeis, in the same smooth voice. 'Will you take a cheque?'

He extracted a leather-bound chequebook and a pen, and scrawled. Then he handed a cheque to Professor Carlyle.

'Will this do?' he said. 'I'm sure there must be some equipment your department could usefully use.'

He had been ludicrously extravagant, but so what? The whole world was in rainbow colours.

The professor stared at the cheque, his eyes widening, then stared at the very expensive car occupying his parking space, then at Alexeis, and then at Carrie, still hooked into Alexeis's arm. His myopic eyes narrowed.

'He seems filthy rich. Are you going to marry him?' he said.

'Yes,' said Alexeis.

'Good,' said Professor Carlyle. 'A rich spouse is always useful in academia! Though I suppose it means biochemistry will get his patronage. I'll bank this while I can, I think!' He popped the cheque into his battered tweed jacket. 'Well, young man, don't just stand there—get that monstrosity out of my space. And, however much money you've got to throw around insufficiently funded university departments, don't do it again!'

'Certainly not, Professor,' Alexeis assured him, heading for his car. He paused, and turned his head. 'Professor, I wonder—can you tell me? I happen to be marrying an exceptionally clever woman, as clever as she is beautiful, and I want to impress her by telling her I know the chemical formula for the extremely large diamond I wish to buy her for our engagement.'

'What?' barked the Professor. 'Just how stupid are you, young man? It's C for carbon! You won't impress her by knowing that!'

'No,' said Alexeis chastened. 'I'll just have to find some other way of impressing her.'

'Tell her you love her,' said the Professor dryly. 'It worked in my day…'

Alexeis smiled. 'Excellent advice,' he agreed. 'Thank you.' He handed Carrie into the car, then came round to his side and got in beside her. He hooked his hand around Carrie's nape and drew her to him.

'I love you, Dr Carrie Richards—Nicolaides-to-be,' he said softly. 'Now and for ever and all our days together, with all my heart and all my soul. And even—' his eyes glinted '—with my highly inferior brain.'

'Idiot,' said Carrie. But there was a break in her voice. Happiness greater than she had ever known was rolling in waves through her. She reached for Alexeis's hand and clutched it tightly.

'I love you too,' she whispered.

'Good,' said Alexeis. 'That just proves how smart you really are.'

Then he kissed her.

Behind him, the professor of geological sciences started exasperatedly tooting his horn.

But inside Alexeis's car, Carrie only heard violins soaring.

EPILOGUE

CARRIE stood at the top of the imposing oak staircase that led down into the hall below. Although in darkness, the dying embers of the fire in the stone fireplace gave a warm glow to the room, catching the glitter of ornaments on the Christmas tree that towered to the ceiling. She leant against the carved balustrade and gave a sigh of happiness. Although she was clad only in a silky peignoir, the Victorian mansion Alexeis had bought for them in the depths of the countryside outside Marchester was toast-warm.

Footsteps sounded along the landing. Carrie's head turned and, as it always did, her stomach gave a little quiver to see the tall, powerful figure of Alexeis, still in his tuxedo, but with his collar undone and tie loose, strolling purposefully towards her. But now it was not just her stomach that flipped when she saw him in all his gorgeousness—her heart flipped too. And her breath caught—love flowing into the space around her heart, eyes softening even as her pulse quickened.

He saw her expression and his answered hers as he came to her and put his arms around her supple waist. She gave a little sigh of contentment and caught his strong forearms.

'My beautiful Carrie.' He smiled, and dropped a kiss on her head. 'Time for bed,' he said. Then he turned to look down into the hall below. 'It went well, I think,' he said. There was a note of satisfaction in his voice.

Carrie smiled. 'Yes, I think it did,' she agreed. 'And I have to say—' her voice became mischievous '—you make a splendid baron, entertaining in your very own baronial hall!'

His gaze dropped to Carrie. 'You are happy here?' he asked. There was a questioning note in his voice that moved her.

'I love it,' she said indulgently. 'And I loved our very first Christmas party here! And I loved the way you were happy to invite the whole biochem department—'

'They are your colleagues—of course I would invite them! Even if—' he made a bit of a face '—I couldn't understand most of what they were talking about.'

He lowered his head and kissed her lips.

'And I, my adored Carrie, am happier than I thought it was ever possible for a man to be. I have all that I could desire—all that I could ever want. You—my love, my heart, the meaning of my life.'

He wrapped her tight against him and she gave a little choke. How could she ever have thought she didn't love him? How could she ever have thought she didn't need him to be with her, all her life?

How did I ever think he was only a fantasy—when he's the most real, most precious person in all the world to me?

Sadness tinged her wonder. Though Alexeis had swept her away into a fantasy, now he was part of the core reality of her life—making himself at home in her rarefied world as though he had always been there, giving up without regret his globe-trotting lifestyle to be with her.

'I wish my father could have met you,' she murmured wistfully. 'I wish he were still here. But I am glad—glad with all my heart—that now I have your mother in my life, welcoming me into yours.'

'Didn't I tell you she would? And didn't I also tell you…' his eyes glinted in a way that made Carrie's stomach flip again, and his arm tightened around her '…that it was time for bed?'

With a decisive action he scooped her up, silk peignoir trailing to the floor, and strode off down the landing to their bedroom. Carrie clung to him as he swept her off to bed.

'And did I tell you…' his long, long lashes swept down over his eyes as he lowered her to the bed beneath him, her hair streaming like a banner across the pillows '…how very, very much I love you, Dr Nicolaides?'

She hooked her hands around his neck, fingers spearing into his dark, silky hair.

'About a million times,' she whispered, gazing up at him, lovelight in her face. 'But don't stop telling me.'

'All my days,' he promised her. 'And definitely…very, very definitely…' he started to kiss her tender mouth with soft, seductive caresses that turned her body to a glowing flame '…all my nights…'

* * * * *

Here's a sneak peek at
THE CEO'S CHRISTMAS PROPOSITION,
the first in USA TODAY *bestselling author*
Merline Lovelace's HOLIDAYS ABROAD *trilogy*
coming in November 2008.

American Devon McShay is about to get the Christmas
surprise of a lifetime when she meets her new client,
sexy billionaire Caleb Logan, for the very first time.

Silhouette®
Desire

Available November 2008

Her breath whistled out in a sigh of relief when he exited Customs. Devon recognized him right away from the newspaper and magazine articles her friend and partner Sabrina had looked up during her frantic prep work.

Caleb John Logan, Jr. Thirty-one. Six-two. With jet-black hair, laser-blue eyes and a linebacker's shoulders under his charcoal-gray cashmere overcoat. His jaw-dropping good looks didn't score him any points with Devon. She'd learned the hard way not to trust handsome heartbreakers like Cal Logan.

But he was a client. An important one. And she was willing to give someone who'd served a hitch in the marines before earning a B.S. from the University of Oregon, an MBA from Stanford and his first million at the ripe old age of twenty-six the benefit of the doubt.

Right up until he spotted the hot-pink pashmina, that is.

Devon knew the flash of color was more visible than the sign she held up with his name on it. So she wasn't surprised when Logan picked her out of the crowd and cut in her direction. She'd just plastered on her best businesswoman smile when he whipped an arm around her waist. The next moment she was sprawled against his cashmere-covered chest.

"Hello, brown eyes."

Swooping down, he covered her mouth with his.

Sheer astonishment kept Devon rooted to the spot for a few seconds while her mind whirled chaotically. Her first thought was that her client had downed a few too many drinks during the long flight. Her second, that he'd mistaken the kind of escort and consulting services her company provided. Her third shoved everything else out of her head.

The man could kiss!

His mouth moved over hers with a skill that ignited sparks at a half dozen flash points throughout her body. Devon hadn't experienced that kind of spontaneous combustion in a while. A *long* while.

The sparks were still popping when she pushed off his chest, only now they fueled a flush of anger.

"Do you always greet women you don't know with a lip-lock, Mr. Logan?"

A smile crinkled the skin at the corners of his eyes. "As a matter of fact, I don't. That was from Don."

"Huh?"

"He said he owed you one from New Year's Eve two years ago and made me promise to deliver it."

She stared up at him in total incomprehension. Logan hooked a brow and attempted to prompt a nonexistent memory.

"He abandoned you at the Waldorf. Five minutes before midnight. To deliver twins."

"I don't have a clue who or what you're…"

Understanding burst like a water balloon.

"Wait a sec. Are you talking about Sabrina's old boyfriend? Your buddy, who's now an ob-gyn doc?"

It was Logan's turn to look startled. He recovered faster than Devon had, though. His smile widened into a rueful grin.

"I take it you're not Sabrina Russo."

"No, Mr. Logan, I am not."

* * * * *

Be sure to look for
THE CEO'S CHRISTMAS PROPOSITION
by Merline Lovelace.
Available in November 2008 wherever books are sold,
including most bookstores, supermarkets,
drugstores and discount stores.

Exclusively His

Back in his bed—and he's better than ever!

Whether you shared his bed for one night—
or five years—certain men are impossible to forget!
He might be your ex, but when you're back in his bed,
the passion is not just hot, it's scorching!

Things get tricky for sensible Veronica when
she unexpectedly meets Lucien again after one
night in Paris. And now he's determined to
seduce her back into his bed....

PUBLIC SCANDAL, PRIVATE MISTRESS
by **Susan Napier**
#2777

Available in November.

*Look out for more Exclusively His novels
in Harlequin Presents in 2009!*

I ♥

HARLEQUIN *Presents*

BROUGHT TO YOU BY FANS OF
HARLEQUIN PRESENTS.

We are its editors and authors
and biggest fans—and we'd
love to hear from YOU!

Subscribe today to our online blog at
www.iheartpresents.com

REQUEST YOUR FREE BOOKS!

 HARLEQUIN *Presents*

PASSION GUARANTEED SEDUCTION

2 FREE NOVELS PLUS 2 FREE GIFTS!

YES! Please send me 2 FREE Harlequin Presents® novels and my 2 FREE gifts (gifts are worth about $10). After receiving them, if I don't wish to receive any more books, I can return the shipping statement marked "cancel". If I don't cancel, I will receive 6 brand-new novels every month and be billed just $4.05 per book in the U.S. or $4.74 per book in Canada, plus 25¢ shipping and handling per book and applicable taxes, if any*. That's a savings of close to 15% off the cover price! I understand that accepting the 2 free books and gifts places me under no obligation to buy anything. I can always return a shipment and cancel at any time. Even if I never buy another book, the two free books and gifts are mine to keep forever.

106 HDN ERRW 306 HDN ERRL

Name	(PLEASE PRINT)	
Address		Apt. #
City	State/Prov.	Zip/Postal Code

Signature (if under 18, a parent or guardian must sign)

Mail to the **Harlequin Reader Service:**
IN U.S.A.: P.O. Box 1867, Buffalo, NY 14240-1867
IN CANADA: P.O. Box 609, Fort Erie, Ontario L2A 5X3

Not valid to current subscribers of Harlequin Presents books.

Want to try two free books from another line?
Call 1-800-873-8635 or visit www.morefreebooks.com.

* Terms and prices subject to change without notice. N.Y. residents add applicable sales tax. Canadian residents will be charged applicable provincial taxes and GST. Offer not valid in Quebec. This offer is limited to one order per household. All orders subject to approval. Credit or debit balances in a customer's account(s) may be offset by any other outstanding balance owed by or to the customer. Please allow 4 to 6 weeks for delivery. Offer available while quantities last.

Your Privacy: Harlequin Books is committed to protecting your privacy. Our Privacy Policy is available online at www.eHarlequin.com or upon request from the Reader Service. From time to time we make our lists of customers available to reputable third parties who may have a product or service of interest to you. If you would prefer we not share your name and address, please check here. ☐

HP08R

HARLEQUIN *Presents*

EXTRA

MARRIED BY CHRISTMAS

For better or worse—she'll be his by Christmas!

As the festive season approaches, these darkly handsome Mediterranean men are looking forward to unwrapping their brand-new brides…. Whether they're living luxuriously in London or flying by private jet to their glamorous European villas, these arrogant, commanding tycoons need a wife…and they'll have one—by Christmas!

HIRED: THE ITALIAN'S CONVENIENT MISTRESS
by CAROL MARINELLI (Book #29)

THE SPANISH BILLIONAIRE'S CHRISTMAS BRIDE
by MAGGIE COX (Book #30)

CLAIMED FOR THE ITALIAN'S REVENGE
by NATALIE RIVERS (Book #31)

THE PRINCE'S ARRANGED BRIDE
by SUSAN STEPHENS (Book #32)

Happy holidays from Harlequin Presents!

Available in November.

Coming Next Month

Plus, look out for the fabulous new collection *Married by Christmas* in Harlequin Presents® EXTRA: